I0551670

WILL

STEELE RIDERS MC 2ND GENERATION
BOOK 1

C.M. STEELE

THE STEELE PRESS

ISBN: 978-1-954645-22-6

Like father, like son, William Steele knows what he wants, and he'll stop at nothing to claim it. Fierce, loyal, and relentless, he's set his sights on the one woman who owns his heart. There's just one problem: Melanie is Beast's daughter and the well-dressed DA didn't earn that moniker ironically. The man was extremely protective of his family.

Winning her love is one thing. Earning her father's respect? That's a battle in itself. But as the future president of the Riders Will is no stranger to pressure, and no Rider walks away from the woman meant to be his.

Yet the real danger isn't the man guarding her. It's the shadow creeping closer, a threat determined to shatter their future before it even begins. As enemies close in and loyalties are tested, he will have to prove that nothing, not family, not fear, not even fate, can stand between a Rider and his woman.

CHAPTER ONE

WILL

"Melanie," I gasp, waking up covered in a cold sweat and shooting straight up in my bed. I feel around in the darkness, but I'm all alone. It was just a dream—a painfully erotic dream about my long-time friend who has captivated me far longer than I care to admit. The sun isn't even up yet, so I take off my tee shirt, swipe the sweat off my face and chest, and lie back down.

My heart's going to pop out of my chest, and I know it.

There is a damn complicated yet perfectly explainable reason for this bullshit, and her name is Melanie Brandon. She is my little raven, with eyes that I could drown in and a smile that captures my fantasies.

Fuck, it's hot in the Texas summer heat, but that's not the reason why I'm burning up. Melanie has me on fire, aching for her with a lust that's undeniable. She's three years younger than me, and yet it feels like we're a million years apart. I have to wait one more year before I can make her mine, and I will, but the time apart has been endless. The long, lonely nights have become longer.

My dad was right, and it finally hits me. "Finally" isn't the right word because it hit me too soon. Way too damn soon. I've got a long way to go before I can make her mine.

Fuck, I'm in trouble. This road has been a long one, longer than anything I've come across so far, and it's not over yet. My dad thought he had it bad when he fell in love with my mom, but it was nothing compared to my love for Melanie.

I jumped out of bed and hit the floor, palms flat, toes pointed down and stomach on the ground. "One," I grunt. "Two." The push-ups drive me on until I've done a hundred and collapse on the floor. My arms burn, body dripping with more sweat.

At least my hard-on has faded, and my arms are too sore to beat my cock to death. It's the only thing keeping the fucker from being completely raw. I'd stroked it to numbness while I was away at college. Being back home for summer break isn't any better, but work and friends make it a little easier to deal with seeing Melanie even in passing.

Scrambling back onto my feet, I hit the pull-up bar next. I work out for the next two hours, getting my body primed and ready before I go to see the love of my life today.

I pop in the shower to wash off all the grime and then step out to shave. It takes another twenty minutes before I'm dressed in a pair of jeans and a plain white tee. The sun is going to be baking outside today, but I'll be on my ride, so I prefer my jeans. Stopping in my small kitchen, I scarf down some breakfast.

I'm almost outside my front door when my cell rings. Pulling it out my pocket, I answer it just before it goes to voicemail. "What's up, Pops?"

"Just calling to check on you." I wonder what else is on his mind. We see each other every single day and I work with him for ten damn hours.

"I'm just heading out on my way over to the clubhouse. In fact, I'm riding my new motorcycle there.

"Cool. Tell me how it is." It was a gift for my birthday, and I haven't had a chance to truly enjoy it since I went back to school, so this will be my opportunity.

"I will."

"You're going to behave today, right?" he asks. I knew there had to be a reason for this call.

"What's that supposed to mean?"

"Melanie's going to be here, and...she's not quite an adult."

"I know, Pops. Trust me. I haven't forgotten." Today, I'll let her know that she has a year to prepare for her future. I have no plans to stop her from fulfilling her dreams of becoming a librarian like her mother was, but that doesn't mean that our future won't begin when she turns eighteen,

3

which unfortunately isn't until next summer. A whole brutal year away.

"She'll probably be dressed up and there will be other guys who are not related."

"They know where I stand, so I expect them to act accordingly and then so will I. Trust me when I say that I have learned to control my jealousy. I trust my cousins to look after her."

"Okay. I'll see you later." I end the call and tuck my phone away before hopping on my bike and revving it up.

Driving onto the main road, I take a long ride, passing by Melanie's home. I don't know what I expected to happen, but no one is outside because they're either getting ready or already there, so I ride to the party.

"Hey, future Prez," Dusty says as he opens the gate. He's about ten years older than me, slender with shaggy, sandy brown hair.

"Hey. Who is this?" I nod to the guy beside him. This guy seems to be about my age with a medium build, well-defined, handsome fucker that I don't want around my woman. His jet-black hair is cut short, nearly faded to his scalp, making him look dangerous. I immediately don't like him.

"He's new. This is Damon." He points to Damon and says, "Damon, this is Will Steele, Boomer's son."

"It's a pleasure to meet you, Prez." His eyes traveled over me and my motorcycle, inspecting me. "Damn, that's a killer bike."

"Thanks." My tone is flat because I don't need his approval or want it. I've got an uncomfortable vibe from him. The tension just rolls off his shoulders as he stares. Where the fuck did they get this asshole?

"Yeah, you got that as a birthday present, right?" Dusty says, just trying to ease the tension building.

"Damn, that must be nice." I want to snap his fucking neck right here. He's so fucking lucky I wouldn't make a scene when the Steele Rider wives put so much effort in making this party wonderful.

"It was time for my old one to retire for parts. I'll see you later, Dusty." I drive in, ignoring the new fuck because that was clearly a dick comment full of jealousy and a lack of understanding. It wasn't like I couldn't afford my own motorcycle since I work as well as go to school.

My entire existence has led to this point—following in my father's footsteps and becoming his successor as the head of the Steele Riders and the future head of this town. We have no mayor, but we do have organizations to help keep the town running smoothly. Since there are only three thousand people, we don't need empty figureheads. Property owners and police regulate most of the issues, and the rest of the problems and regulations are handled by the Steele Riders.

Although I'm only twenty years old, I've been under an apprenticeship of one kind or another since I was eight, getting ready to lead the next generation into the fold. Now, all I need is my queen by my side.

I pull into my personal spot away from the party area—the clubhouse that has grown since my father started the club before he met my mother. It's larger in size, and the yard has been remodeled to make it a better picnic area for the many kids that have grown up alongside the Steele Riders.

As I turn off my engine, I see my brother Eddie. "Hey, Will, there you are. Come on. Mom and Dad are already here and so are half the guests, including Mel." I shush him and wave my hand to tamp down his voice. I'm not embarrassed about my feelings for Melanie in the least, but her father is a bigger issue. He's my uncle, for all intents and purposes. I grew up with all the Riders as surrogate uncles, so he won't be pleased with the news that I want to screw his little girl. Granted, I want so much more, but I'm sure that's all he'd see.

My brother and I walk together, entering the fray, and even though I may not look it, my eyes are scanning for my future wife. There is no way I can keep my eyes from finding her. It isn't like she's hard to spot: five four, long black hair that shines in the sun like onyx. I groan, thinking about running my fingers through it, fisting it while bringing her lips to mine for a deep, penetrative kiss.

"How about I grab you a drink?" he asks.

"Sounds good," I choke out, clearing my throat. My eyes linger a little too long, but then I turn back to my brother and smile. "I'm going to say hi to a couple of people."

"Like Mel?" he teases.

"No. Now isn't the time." He looks at me like I have two heads, but the kid has no idea what this pain in my gut is like. As much as I want to be so close to her, like a second skin, it's impossible. If I did, I'd never leave. I'd pull her into my arms and do unspeakable things to those plump lips that part so sweetly when she laughs or smiles.

"Yeah, because ignoring the woman who means the most to you is really going to endear her to you. I might be young, but I'm not an idiot. You don't want other guys sniffing around her. She's gorgeous, after all." I growl because my brother's right. He smirks, knowing he's hit the nail right on the head. Before he can come back with a drink, my cousin Daisy brings me a beer.

"Hey, Will, Dad told me to bring this to you. Said you could use it."

"Thanks. Really?" I'm surprised he handed me a beer so soon.

"Yeah, you look tense. Could it have anything to do with my friend and coworker?" she says, tipping her head in Mel's direction. "She's sweet and totally has a super crush on you, although you already know that. Everyone does— well, except her dad, because Beast would probably lose it. Anyway," she adds in a long, drawn-out sigh, "I'm going to go over there. Let me know if you need any help talking to her."

"She's too young for me. We can't have an actual relationship."

"Please." She rolls her eyes. "You're three years apart, and you're both ridiculously mature and lame." She pats my chest and walks away. I shake my head and drink my beer with a chuckle. Just then, my eyes make contact with the woman in question, and my heart nearly stops. I give her a wink, and a blush steals over her pale skin.

I hold my drink to my lips without taking a sip, watching her over the bottle. God, she's grown up to be so beautiful. My eyes never leave her as Melanie Brandon talks to the group of friends and cousins in the corner of the yard where the many Steele Riders and families have gathered. She stands out amongst the girls, as if the sun creates a spotlight right on her long black hair, illuminating her beauty.

I swallow hard, taking a long swig of my now-warm beer as I think about taking her back to my apartment and stripping her out of that tight little yellow sundress that barely kisses her knees that I want to part as I lick my way up to her soft, warm slit, marking it with my tongue until she's screaming my name.

"Will." Beast claps my shoulder, catching me by surprise, and I nearly choke on my beer. "How's it going?" Of all the people to come up to me while I'm obsessing over his daughter. "Looking forward to your final year?"

I take another swig, trying to make it look like I'd been mid drink when he interrupted my light stalking. "Yeah." I swallow.

"Girls?" he asks, brow jerking upward in the familiar way that normally sends people backward in the courtroom. He isn't the typical attorney people expect when they come across the great DA Brandon.

8

"Not really dating," I answer, trying to sound as noncommittal as possible, hoping to keep my feelings from showing for a little while longer.

"Why not?" Thankfully there's no accusation, but I'm still uncomfortable about his line of questioning because I'd just been considering all the ways I want to make his daughter scream my name in every inch of my apartment, my dick throbbing painfully in my jeans.

"I'm focused on my education," I answer.

"Good man. It's better to get it out of the way. Right now, girls are a waste of your time." Is he fucking on to me? He has to be, because that tone screams a warning from a mile away.

I need a distraction, an interruption or some shit because I'm already on edge when it comes to Melanie, and this isn't making it any easier. My dick has been half hard since I walked in, then seeing her sent it into full staff. Luckily it was tucked neatly, mostly hidden, but now her father is interrogating me about my sex life.

Looking for an exit, I turn and see my mother having trouble carrying a large tray. I rush away without a word, but his eyes follow me so I'm sure he understands.

"Thanks, Son," my father says, coming from behind with another set of trays. "She doesn't listen to me."

"I was trying to be helpful," she insists, being stubborn as always, which my father both loves and hates. He worries about her safety all the time.

"There are forty other men here who could have carried the food out after all you women did the damn cooking, Tigress." He swats her ass, and Beast comes up beside his wife, who starts unwrapping the food.

"Nice save, Will," Beast says.

"He's got sharp eyes and will make a great leader one day," my father says. He keeps hinting about my interest in taking over the club. He's worried that my years in college will deter me from becoming the president of his corporation on top of the Steele Riders, but I let him sweat it out. My degree is only to further the club and the business. College will get the police and the Feds off our backs. If we represent ourselves as more law-abiding, college-educated citizens, they tend to let us be. Granted, they have over the years, but when my parents were younger, they did attract a lot of attention. On occasion, they still do.

Last year, we caught some shit when some Colombians came through with the constant influx of migrants. There's no telling the good from the bad these days, and we're left with dog shit on our doorstep to scoop up. The good ones work for us or move on, and the bad ones get sent away or put away, but we can't let the government know that we're not just a humble group of family members riding out on weekends on our bikes.

Suddenly I'm distracted from my task when I hear her musical laughter from a short distance away and turn my head. She's talking to my cousin, and I want to snap his neck. A beefy hand grips my shoulder firmly, squeezing it.

"He knows better already. He's harmless. One more year, Son," my father says in a low whisper near my ear.

"I know, I know. Does Beast know?"

He chuckles in that deep voice that mirrors mine. "You'd know if he did. She's his little girl, so it's not like he'll be happy about it." My father has always had my back even though Beast is one of his closest friends.

"Tell me about it. I swear I got the feeling he caught me staring."

"Maybe he did. Was she alone?" he asks.

"No. For all he knows, I could have been staring at several of the girls or at nothing." I walk away, needing another beer. As I walk to the beer cooler, I nearly collide with Irina, Boss's daughter, and she smiles at me. Beautiful, like all the girls in the club because they take after their mothers, but my heart has always belonged to the most beautiful girl.

"Hey, Will," she gasps, giving me a hug. "How are you?"

When she pulls back, I can see my woman staring at me from behind Irina. "I'm good."

"Your dad said you'd be here today. I had no idea. God, you look incredible, and I hear you're single. You must be beating them off with a stick in college."

"More like beating them with his stick," my cousin Connor says. I don't miss the pure look of disgust on Mel's face at Connor's comment, and I want to punch him in the jaw.

"Speak for yourself," I snarl at him. Snatching a beer from the damn cooler and popping off the bottle cap, I walk away from both of them before I lose my temper.

"Will, where are you..." Connor calls out, but I'm about two seconds from punching him in the mouth. "I didn't mean..." he continues.

"Shut it, Con..." I walk away and head into the clubhouse where I find my little Melanie talking to Doc's son. "Your dad's looking for you, David," I say. He doesn't move fast enough for my liking, so I move closer. "Get the fuck out of here," I grunt with a tilt of my head. As the future president of the Steele Riders, there isn't a single one of them who doesn't already take orders from me, which is good because right now I'm feeling wild.

"Hey, Melanie. How have you been? It's been a long time," I say, suddenly feeling a little less confident than I was with David.

She doesn't look up at me like she did David, which pisses me off. Her eyes focus on the bar top. Her dainty fingernails tease the edge of the surface, nervously digging into the material. "Yeah, it has, although I don't think you've missed me at all since you've been away." When she finishes, her eyes meet mine and there's a look of sadness in them.

I'm surprised by her remark because it's the furthest thing from the truth. Missing her is all I did, besides beat my dick to death with visions of her on my mind. "Why would you say that?"

"Girls at school keeping you busy," she huffs.

I take her busy hands and put them in mine. "Don't fucking believe what Connor said. I've told you what we are."

"You didn't correct him." Her eyes fill with unshed tears.

Damn. I slide her hands into one of mine and then use my other hand to cup her face. "You never gave me a chance to correct him before you stormed off."

She pushes herself away from me and then says, "Look, it's not my business what you do or who you do. Our fathers are friends, and soon I'll be off to college and dating and we'll only see each other on these rare occasions. You'll be the president of the Riders, and I'll be nothing to you but the occasional visitor. A distant memory."

I snag her by the wrist and quickly yank her back to me, sending her chest into mine. The action causes me to lose my breath. Not because it was painful, but having her this close, us touching each other, is more intense than I expected. I quickly release her, giving us the space we both need. Melanie might pretend that she's unfazed, but her body's pulse races in my arms, her pupils dilate, and her chest rises and falls with devastated longing.

After a moment, I found my words. "That's not true, Melanie. Next year, we'll be getting ready to start our life together."

"What makes you believe that?" she questions.

"Because we're obsessed with each other."

"What makes you think I feel the same way?" I love that spicy challenge. Her hazel eyes brighten with fire as she dares me.

I move in closer, my hands on either side of her, pinning her to the bar. "I overheard your conversation with your friend. She dared you to admit that you loved me and wanted to have my babies. You finally said you did, but that it would never happen because there was no way I could see you as anything more than a friend." She gasps and pales. I don't let her get away with it because I understand that she's afraid to admit the truth. "Friendship is the last thing on my mind when I see you, but you'll understand next year when I graduate and make you mine."

"Don't lie to me, Will." She waves her hands around. She wants proof, and I'll give it to her. Fisting her hair, I bring my face close to hers and then trail my nose along her throat while my hips press along hers. "Can you feel what you do to me, my sweet, dark-haired raven? What I want? I want to be buried so deep inside of you that we can't ever be separated."

Her legs hook around my waist, and her hands slide into my hair. I grind a little harder, licking her throat before biting down. I'm so damn close to nutting, but I won't do that to her.

"Rett," she gasps as my lips trail over her pulse. Fuck. She hasn't called me that in so damn long—since the time I found her at the lake with the other kids and she was in a tiny bikini. I'd been so damn jealous.

"Lanie, be careful. Calling me that is going to get you fucked right here, right now." There's a noise at the metal club door, reminding us that there's an entire party outside. "Damn it." I step away from the love of my life, giving us a little space, our breathing labored.

She pales and stares at the door, refusing to meet my gaze again. "I've got to go. I promised Penny that I'd work at the bakery today. It was good to see you, so maybe we'll see each other sometime soon. If not, best of luck in college." She moves right past me and out of my sight before I can think of a reason to stop her. Damn, she's fucking fast. I know she runs track at school, but hell, I never expected her to dash away from me like that.

I polish off another beer before I step back out to the yard where everyone is gathered, and Beast has his eyes on me. Right now, I don't give a fuck because I'm pissed, horny, and frustrated.

He pulls me aside and says, "We need to talk."

"Yes, Sir."

Beast runs his hand through his thick hair angrily. "When I asked you about girls, you conveniently left out my daughter."

"What was I supposed to say? It's not like we're a couple yet. She's not eighteen, and I have one more year in school before I come home."

"How long has this been going on?"

"My feelings have always been there, but I've never crossed the line." Okay, that's a bit of a lie.

"Not from what I saw." My eyes widen.

"Excuse me?"

"Who the fuck do you think knocked on the door when I found my daughter wrapped up in your arms? I gave her a chance to untangle herself before I came barging in."

"It wasn't what you think. I was the one who…"

"I know what I saw. My baby had her legs wrapped around you while you had your hands elsewhere. Luckily I could see those fuckers too, or we'd have a problem."

"Look—I just wanted to explain to her that my plans were to eventually make her my wife."

"You know she's my little girl."

"Any woman I marry will be someone's little girl. I want Melanie and only Melanie."

"Until it's time, give her the space she needs to grow, and if she wants you, then I won't interfere. But, if she chooses otherwise, I'll stand by my daughter. Do you understand me, Will?" He gives me a stern glare, warning me that he won't be intimidated.

"Yes, but she feels the same way I do. I know it, and obviously you do too." I'm pressing my luck when he stands straighter, nostrils flaring.

"I'm not saying you're wrong, but you're both stubborn and it's not time for this debate. She still has a lot of growing up to do."

"Fine. I have a lot to do, anyway." My plan is to keep her well-guarded while I'm gone. Who can I put on her? I consider my options and the person that comes to mind. He is close in age but has a girlfriend that he's obsessed with, so he'll do just fine. After taking a deep breath, I lock myself in my father's office to make the call and square away my business. Finally, I calm down and return to the party.

In one more year, little Melanie Brandon will be mine and everyone will know it.

CHAPTER TWO

MELANIE

DASHING OUT OF THE CLUBHOUSE MIGHT NOT HAVE BEEN THE brightest idea because I hadn't bothered to check my appearance and who might be around. Looking down to see if my tits are showing, I slam right into my father. "Dad," I gasp, as his hands wrap around my biceps.

"Princess." He looks me over and adds, "Please tell me I don't have to kill him."

"No, of course not," I answer, grateful that my boobs are perfectly covered.

"He didn't hurt you, break your heart…. take things where you didn't want," he adds, brushing my hair back behind my ears.

"How…what?" I ask, stammering and taking a step back. How the hell did he know what we were doing?

"I walked in there looking for your mother when I saw you two."

"Oh God. Nothing happened. I swear, Daddy. It's just maybe a too friendly hug."

He grumbles under his breath. *Too friendly hug, my ass.* He clears his throat and stares at me with a raised brow, crossing his arms. "If you didn't see me, why did you run out?"

"Because I'm confused about his intentions. Look, I have to go help at the bakery. I have to go. Can we not talk about this later?"

He drops his tough stance, giving me that sigh, telling me I've won for now. "You can talk about this with your mother tomorrow."

"Okay. Thank you, Daddy." I kiss his cheek.

"Good. I love you, Princess."

"I love you too. I even love Will." I leave him with that so he doesn't end up fighting him. As close as they are, I'd hate for my father to act after what he saw. God, my father saw me climbing Will like a tree.

My bestie is going to give me a ride, so she should be here any minute. I give her a call and walk toward the exit of the lot. "Hey, Beth. Where are you?"

"I'm outside the gate, talking to the prospects. Meet me out here, girlie. One of them is really cute."

"Whatever. I'm coming." She knows all I care about is

Will. I exit through the door, and she's there talking to Dusty and a guy I don't know. "Hey, are you ready?"

"Sure, but say hi to Damon. Damon, this is Melanie. Isn't she absolutely gorgeous?" my best friend gushes, grabbing me by the arm and dragging me closer to the prospects. My tits bounce more than I'd care for them to, giving them a better look at my curves. I flush with embarrassment, thinking about how I only dressed this way for Will to see me. Now this man has clearly gotten his an eyeful and likes what he sees.

"So damn hot," he says under his breath.

"She's Beast's daughter," Dusty warns him. I want to add that I'm Will's woman, but I'm still hesitant to play that card. That would be too much too soon.

"She's old enough to date, though," Beth adds. Damn it, girl. I want to scream at her, but I control myself because I'd just been caught and I'm not old enough to even be intimate with Will yet.

"Yes, but…" I'm about to answer when my father steps out of the door.

"You're still here, Princess. You should be off to work before you're late."

"I'm going. Beth was introducing me to the new prospect."

"Oh yeah," he says with a suspicious tone in his voice as he looks over the new guy. "Well, I'm not sure Will would appreciate it. You're dating now, so they'll learn to keep their eyes and hands to themselves. Isn't that right, fellas?"

Dusty is quick to answer, "Yes, Sir." It takes a moment for Damon to follow up with a yes. My father gives him a look that makes me nervous, but I don't have time to judge. I'm already pushing the time limit.

"Let's go, or I'm going to be late and Penny's not going to make it to the party."

I make it there in ten minutes and Penny smiles, leaving me there as she runs out with her husband, who thanks us for taking over. Even though the town is small, the bakery is extremely popular and the only one in town. I get to work and spend the rest of the evening working and doing my best to keep my mind off Will which is pointless because the man lives there rent free with his own mansion and man cave.

CHAPTER THREE

WILL

THE DAY HAS GONE FROM LOUSY TO SHITTY SINCE I WOKE UP this morning, but I know there's one thing that will make it better. Tearing the door open, I rush into the steel container and close the door, pacing. I've been avoiding this call because my willpower when it comes to her is almost zero, but I need to hear her voice.

It's been two days since the barbeque, but I have to give Melanie a call because I can't wait to speak to her. I gave her some space to let her think about what happened in the clubhouse, but I refuse to allow her time to deny the truth. The phone rings four times and I'm almost afraid she won't pick up, but then on the last ring she does. "Good afternoon, Melanie."

"Hello, Will," she answers and the sound of my heart in my ears starts to slow down.

"No 'Rett'?" I questioned as I relax. Plopping down onto my desk chair, toss my feet on my temporary desk.

"I thought you warned me about that?" she answers with a bit of sauciness that goes straight to my dick. I groan and regret being in this position.

"Well, I'd say we're a safe distance apart." Although I would say she's never a safe distance away from me. Hearing her voice is an instant turn on for me.

"Yes. Well, let's just say it's for special occasions." That's good because when she calls me Rhett, I picture the way she wrapped around me, aching to come.

"I can live with that," I choke out. Clearing my throat, I ask, "How are you doing?"

"A little tired since I just finished another shift at the bakery."

Checking the time on my phone, it's only one. "Already?"

"Yes. I opened up at four this morning."

I'm on my feet, pacing with annoyance. A growl rips from my throat. She's working too damn hard. "What the hell? I'm going to have a talk with my aunt and uncle."

She giggles on the other end. "No, you won't. It's my job, and I don't mind. Besides, it's only for the summer, and since I don't have anything else to do, it occupies my time. What are you doing with your time?" Her tone shifts, and I read it clear as day. My baby girl is jealous as fuck, but she doesn't have a reason because she has all of me.

24

I smiled, wishing she was in front of me because she'd know damn well that she had nothing to worry about. "I've been at work since five. I'm taking a break to call my beautiful woman. I've missed you, Lanie."

"How come you don't call me Mel like everyone else?"

"Because everyone else does." One time my cousin called her Mel, and I punched him in the gut with a warning that she's only Mel to me and me alone.

"Of course. It's so you," she answers with another soft giggle, and I fight my arousal, adjusting myself in my jeans. I'm grateful I took the call in the construction trailer instead of outside or in my work truck because I don't need an audience.

"What are we?"

"We're—" My answer is cut off by a pounding on my trailer door.

I'm about to answer it when it bursts open. "Boss, we have a problem out in section seven in zone four. We need you," my foreman says, storming into the office. "One of the beams fell. Two men were injured."

"Baby, I have to go." I ended the call, wishing I could continue talking and reassuring her that everything I do is for her and our future.

It wasn't until ten at night when I got home. After the trip to the hospital to make sure my crew members were okay and everything at the site was handled, I hit my apartment to shower. All I can think about is hearing Melanie's voice, but I can't go there because I'll beg her to come here and ease the frustration rushing through my sore bones. Her father may approve of us being together, but not of me fucking her.

I jump into the shower and wash off the sweat and stress from my body as best as I can. When I finally climb out, I crash onto my bed and fall into a fitful sleep.

Morning comes too soon, but the first thing I do is send the woman I love is a text message.

> Raven, you're a dangerous temptation. I'm going to miss you but know that I'm not far away and I'm always watching. Yes, we're a couple. I'm working non-stop because I lost two men who were injured on a worksite today. I have to keep my distance, but that doesn't mean I won't be thinking of you.

IT'S TIME TO HEAD BACK TO SCHOOL AND I'M ACTUALLY grateful because I'm fucking exhausted from my long days and grueling work. Despite being back in Steeleville, I didn't feel like I was home. Maybe it was the fact that I had to avoid the only reason for coming home, my Melanie.

My parents were glaring at me as I sat at their kitchen table. "What?"

"You're not going to say goodbye to her before you go?"

"No. It's not a good idea."

"Why?" my mother asked, looking so heartbroken. She has no idea what it's already doing to me. Does she know that I'd lose my will to leave if I saw that similar look on Melanie's face? The same look I saw on my Raven's face when I watched her from across the street from the bakery last week. My mind goes right back there and all I can think of is the last time I saw my love for her.

I had to stop in town to pick up some tools when I drove past the bakery and I'd been a glutton, needing a glimpse of my Melanie. There was a chance she was working, so I looked for her car and there was the dark blue vehicle. Sneaking a peek, I saw her long dark hair up in a bun, strands falling out the sides, adding to her beauty. Growling and groaning like a fool on the side of the road.

Chrissy from the salon spotted my perusal and I knew it was time to move on before she got any closer. "Don't come any closer because I'm not sure I won't snap your neck," I growl.

Hopping back in my truck, I drove off to do my job and regret that I still have a long time before we can truly be together.

"Earth to Will," my dad says, snapping his fingers in front of my face. I shake my head and blink my eyes several times.

"Sorry about that."

"You were lost in thought?"

"A memory of Melanie as always. It's why it took so long to finish some of the projects. Honestly, I have to keep myself focused on work and school because I can't be near her without wanting to touch her."

"Is this all about sex?" my mother asks, frowning with disappointment on her sweet face. My father's mouth drops and I'm stunned for a moment and a bit ashamed.

"Mother," I sigh. I run my hands through my hair.

"Tigress, that's not cool."

"No, it's not all about that, but I've waited for her, so it's not like I don't have urges and the only woman I want is her."

"So you want to be with her and every time you see or touch her, it's instant arousal," my father fills in the rest.

"I love her. I want her happiness above all. Distance is the best I can do. She can decide her fate, but I let every asshole in town know she's mine. When I come back we can move on together. I don't need to add to the neediness. If she keeps busy with other things she won't think about me as much. It's the reason I work myself to the bone."

"It's cute, son. It won't work, but she does need to focus on her school work and friends for the rest of the year, so I'll make sure she's doing that."

"Thank you." I give her a kiss and a hug and then give my father a hug before hopping into my SUV and heading off to school.

I send a message to my woman with a promise. One that both turns me on and sets my teeth on edge. I hate that there's a chance anyone could hit on my woman while I'm gone. Doubling her security is an option, but then there will be more men around her.

She's safe in Steeleville, so I don't ask for more protection, but I will have people looking in on her, just not that piece of shit Damon. I want that asshole as far away from her as possible. I won't admit it because everyone will just say I'm acting like a jealous weak man, but I hate him.

CHAPTER FOUR

MELANIE

I step into the only hair salon in town, hating this place more than usual. The salon isn't my thing because my hair is long, sleek, and dark black. There's no reason for me to change the color. Also, I've despised this place since they added Chrissy Benson to their list of stylists. She's a bitch who thinks that every available man in town should be hers, including William Steele—my Will.

"Hey, Mel, come on over here." Maria pats the salon chair with a big smile. Maria's a different person completely and a doll. "What can I do for you today?"

"You know she's not going to get anything done but a cut." I hate her and her smartass comments.

"Well, that's because she has a naturally beautiful color and doesn't have to change it," Mrs. Steele says, tipping her head to the side with a smile as she sits in a chair beside me while getting highlights.

I blush because William's mother has always been sweet to me. And after what happened at the barbeque two months ago, I've felt uncomfortable around his family just in case he'd said something or didn't. Frankly, I don't know where we stand. Since our phone call was cut short, we haven't spoken to each other. He sent me a text explaining that we were a couple, but he was going to be working nonstop until he left for school again.

Then, the last day before school, he sent me another message.

> Behave, my raven. I'm watching, and I'll know. The second you turn eighteen, I'll make you pay for all your transgressions. I'll miss you and will visit during Christmas break. Be a good girl, and I'll give you your present early.

I almost want to piss him off and be a bad girl, but it's not who I am. Besides, my dad would lose his shit and probably kill any man that comes around me. I consider dying my hair, getting some highlights, or doing something wild that would freak him out, but I pass. I love it when he calls me Raven. "I wanted to take off some length and touch up my bangs."

"Sounds good." It doesn't take Maria long to clean me up. As I go to pay the bill, she stops me. "Your tab is taken care of."

"What?"

Mrs. Steele winks at me. I try to give her a tip, but she stops me.

"We're good, and by the way—you look fabulous." I blush again, adding more color to my rounded face. The bangs add a dimension to me that I love. "I need a pic to add to my website." She grins and snaps a quick couple of shots before I can argue. Smiling, she gives me a hug.

The timer goes off. "Sorry, I have to get these off before I get in trouble." She grits her teeth and walks with Mrs. Steele to the wash stations. I wave to both ladies before leaving. Chrissy gives me a dirty look, rolling her eyes as I pass her station.

"DAD, WHY ARE THERE EXTRA GUARDS ON ME?"

"No more than any of the other young girls in the family," he mutters. We all have a level of security.

"That's not true, and you know it. Is there something you're not telling me? Do you have a dangerous case or something?"

"No. I'm telling you that you're completely safe and they're just looking after you. So, have you filled out your college applications?" I want to say that I have no interest in college, but my father is so successful, and he'd be disappointed in me if I wasn't going to school. What I really want is Will to come back and keep his promise, but how can I believe it? It's almost Christmas, and I haven't heard a word from him. Not even a simple text. He can't be that busy unless girls are keeping him occupied. The thought sends my stomach rolling, and I'm immediately nauseous.

I take a look at my phone, pretending to check something before answering, "I have looked into some, but I haven't narrowed any down at the moment."

"Well, then, let me know if you need any help."

"Okay, Daddy." The doorbell rings, and he goes to answer it. When he does, he comes back a moment later, carrying an insanely large red box with a big bow on it.

"Sweetheart, you have an early Christmas present."

"Are you sure it's safe?"

"Yes." My eyes narrow at my overly suspicious father. I rush to the front window, but I'm only quick enough to see the tail end of a very familiar vehicle—Will's.

"Was that Will?" I question.

"Yes, but he had to leave." My heart races and sinks just as fast.

"Of course he did," I sigh, turning my attention to the massive box in the middle of the family room, taking up way too much space when all I want is that jerk who drove away. It's been months since we've seen each other, and he didn't have the decency to even say hello to me. The longer I stare at the red box, I let my frustration at his abandonment fade and wonder what could be in there.

"Well, do you want it now, or should we put it beside the tree?" my father asks, chuckling under his breath.

I whip my head his way, wanting an outlet for my anger. "I have a damn phone, and the man hasn't called me once, and he's only texted me a handful of times."

"You're only seventeen, and he's almost twenty-one. He's lucky that his father's one of my best friends because I know damn well what that man is thinking when he looks at you." A deep heat spreads over my face. "It's best that he keeps his distance, or I might forget my twenty-five-year friendship with Boomer." Oh. Has my father warned Will to stay away from me?

My head twists quickly away toward my gift so he can't read my arousal. "I'll open the present now."

"I'll go in the other room and check on your mother to see if she needs help with dinner." Could this get any more embarrassing?

"Okay." I grab the bow on the massive box that's bigger than me. As I take off the top, the sides come down to reveal a giant, light brown teddy bear wearing a necklace with a diamond book charm. I unclasp the necklace and see that the book opens, and inside is a message written in a beautiful font:

This is just the start of our love story — Will.

I gasp as tears fall from my eyes and I'm unable to fight them back. My mother comes into the room in a mad dash, wiping her hands on a kitchen towel. "Your father just mentioned Will sent you a gift." I turn and look at her with my watery eyes. "Are you okay?"

"Yes. These are happy tears." I show her the necklace, and she smiles.

"Wow, this is beautiful. Do you want me to put it on you?"

"Yes. Please." I lift my hair, and then my mother places it around my neck. Once it's on, I rush to the bathroom to see. It's gorgeous as it sparkles at the top of my breasts right at the top of my cleavage.

I come back out of the bathroom and see my father snarling, crossing his arms like he's furious. "What's wrong?"

"Nothing. Nothing at all." Slowly he begins to smirk to himself and then mutters, "This little stunt is going to backfire on him."

"Don't be so mean," my mother says, swatting at my dad's chest.

"What do you mean?" I ask my father.

"He's trying to put a claim on you earlier than he should, but he doesn't realize how insanely long that necklace is and how low it hangs."

I turn to my mother, wanting her valued opinion. She tips her chin straight at my breasts and then shakes her head. "Your father's not wrong."

I rush to the front hall mirror and look at myself again. I'm wearing a V-neck sweater, and the diamond charm draws attention straight to my ample chest. A lot of attention. That's why my dad was mad. He snarls at men who ogle me and warns them off all the time. This is like a damn beacon. For a man not around, this probably isn't what Will had in mind when he gave it to me.

"Oh, well. I love it."

"You're not going to love it when I start busting heads around town." Maybe I'll have the chain fixed.

"Sweetheart, there's a card in here," my mom says.

"Oh, okay." I take it and sit on the sofa with my knees up to my chest as I open the envelope. They stare at me, waiting impatiently for details, but this is private. "Excuse me." I get to my feet and scoop up my massive bear, lugging it to my bedroom. I can't wait to snuggle into him, thinking of Will.

Merry Christmas, my beautiful Raven,

I wish I could be with you, but I thought I'd leave you with this bear as a temporary replacement until you can lie on my chest every night. We have a long time until then, and trust me when I say that I'm counting down the days. I hope you love your Christmas present.

P.S. I wanted one that fit on the bear's neck without breaking. I know your chain is too long. You have a special necklace waiting for you at Steele Jewelers tomorrow at ten am. — Love, Will.

He loves me. I press the card to my chest, grinning from ear to ear, squealing like a fool. I can't wait to tell Beth, so I call her and she's positively jealous while reminding me that I need to hit the jewelry store and then make sure to stop into the hair salon to brag about my gift from Will.

The next morning, I arrived at Steele Jewelry, which is owned by Mr. Garrett Steele after he couldn't find enough pieces for his wife and decided to have his own shop in town for her. The shop is normally run by some of the Riders. I get there, and it's closed. I'm surprised since I have an appointment.

I knock on the glass pane of the door and just as I do, it opens. "Please come in, Lanie," he whispers, quickly taking my hand and pulling me into the store. He locks it behind me.

"Will," I gasp as my hand and then my chest slam firmly against his broad chest.

"God, I've missed you so much."

"I've missed you too." I look up into those pale blue eyes and swim in them until I watch his gaze fall to my lips. "Are you going to kiss me?"

"I shouldn't."

"Why? It's not like I'm not old enough for a kiss."

"Because it won't stop there. My lips don't only want to taste that pouty, sassy mouth. I want to lick every inch of your skin and feel my way over your entire body," he confesses with a deeper, husky breath. I want that too, but we can't.

"You're right, but I've never been kissed before."

"That's fucking good, because I'd have to kill someone. You belong to me."

"Um, you only told me about this since the barbeque. I could have dated before then."

"No, you couldn't have. I stopped every single one of those assholes from approaching you."

"You what?" I shove at his chest, but he's so strong it takes his willingness to let me go before I break free. He stands in front of the door, so I stomp my foot.

"What was I going to do? Let my future wife go around dating boys that would take orders from me?"

I pace back and forth in the small storefront, trying to process what he said. I've been hit on since I was young, but it never happened more than once. The boy never did it again and would never look my way. "Are you serious?"

"As a motherfucking heart attack."

"For how long?"

"Longer than I care to admit. You're one gorgeous woman, and the male species realizes it."

"You don't want to want me?"

"Sweetheart, I'm not ashamed to want you. I'm pissed that I can't claim you to the world yet. The day you turn eighteen is the day I can shout it out to everyone."

"So, until then, you're kissing and banging whoever you please."

"Melanie, I've been forever faithful to you," he swears. With a possessive stare, he stalks toward me until there isn't an inch of space between us. "You want a kiss? I'll give you one. I can't promise it will be good, but we might as well start somewhere." His mouth slams down on mine, slanting his lips and brushing them over my mouth. It only takes a moment for me to react, and react I do. My hand delves into his hair, tugging as I deepen our kiss. My leg raises, and I gasp when he lifts and cuffs his hand under my knee. The center of him grinds on me as he rolls his pelvis on mine.

"Will," I pant. His other hand goes to my sweater, lifting it until he's cupping my breast. I cry out from the new sensation, grinding on him even harder. My hand reaches down and I grab his belt buckle, but he swiftly pulls back and releases me.

He sets me on my feet and presses his forehead to mine. "Melanie. Fuck. No. No." If I didn't know better by his harsh breathing and racing heart, I'd think he didn't want this. "We can't do this. I've crossed the line, baby girl. You're too damn young for me, and I should hold back a little longer."

I caress his cheek, running my hand along his strong, smooth jaw. He lifts his intense gaze on me, and there's the dark passion in it again. With a growling, "Mine," his mouth dominates me again. My back slams against the wall, shaking the clock, but nothing matters since I need him. I tugged his shirt out of his jeans, running my hand over his lower back.

"We have to stop."

"No," I insist, continuing to ache for more of him and

whatever he's doing to me. The keys in the door draw our attention.

"Get the fuck out of here," he snarls at the door. The person steps back and the keys stop jingling.

"Son, you better fix yourself because I'll be in there in one minute where I will expect an apology."

"Mom, oh my goodness. One moment." He slams his eyes shut while I nearly turn completely red and want to disappear into the ground.

He stares at me and fixes my top, which thankfully wasn't out of place like the first time. I'm more emotionally disheveled than physically. Will turns away from me as he tucks his shirt in and then walks to the door. "Sorry about that, Mom. I thought Ranger was coming in this morning."

"He asked me to open for him. He had an errand to run in Dallas."

"That fucking prick did it on purpose." Will's hands flex in anger. "I'm going to beat his ass for setting me up."

"Don't dare fight with your brother. If he had gotten a peek at your woman, how would you have felt?"

"You saw something?" Oh God. Could this get any more embarrassing?

She shakes her head and gives me a gentle, apologetic smile. Then she glares at her son. "No, but would I have? She's not eighteen, William Garrett Steele." She presses her finger into his chest.

"No, but we started to get carried away."

"Exactly, and you know better than that."

"I know," Will says, sounding completely defeated.

As wrong as it was on his part, I'm just as guilty. "I should go," I say, finally gaining the courage to speak.

"I'm sorry, sweetheart," Mrs. Steele says, coming up to me. "That was rude of me. I'm just so used to being a mother. I won't say a word about this, but I want you both to take care about being alone together."

"It won't happen again," Will says.

"It won't. I promise." I reach for the clasp on my necklace, and Will immediately stops me.

"Perfect—what you came here for. I'd forgotten." Pulling the necklace from the top of the glass case, Will switches the charm on it and then slides behind me. When he sets it over my head, I lift my hair. He lets out a low growl under his breath, leans down, and whispers, "If only we were alone, I'd kiss this beautiful neck."

"I'm only a few feet away, Son," his mother reminds him with an added tut-tut.

"It has to be done right," Will insists. "Is your book facing correctly?"

"Yes, it's perfect," I answered.

"Good." He clasps it and then turns around to face me. "Now it's right where it should be. You better get going before I forget all the reasons I shouldn't kiss you again, my love."

"When will I see you again?"

"I'd like to say soon, but that wouldn't be wise. Be a good girl and know that I'm always with you." He presses his hand to the locket and then opens the store door, nudging me out. I walk away without saying another word and head to my car, which is good because the ass closed the door behind me.

I hear yelling inside and know he's getting chewed out by his mom. Is it because she doesn't approve of me, or just because of the timing? I hope it's the latter. Driving home, my mind races and a big part of me can't wait until my birthday next year.

MONTHS HAVE PASSED WITHOUT A WORD FROM WILL, WHICH I expected but hoped wouldn't happen. Will's lack of contact aches more than it should.

"So, what are you going to do about school?" Beth asks.

"I've already gotten accepted to several schools in the state, and I've decided to stay close. It makes no sense to go far because I'm spoiled rotten by my parents and I'm not ready to move away yet."

"Or you're waiting for Will, and moving across the country would ruin your relationship."

"Even if that were true, why would that be such a big deal? It's not like it matters since I'm getting a degree I can acquire easily around the nation and it's more affordable here."

"True, but you are a bit pathetic when it's for all the wrong reasons."

"I thought you were a fan of Will's."

"I was when he wasn't playing games with you."

I hug her. "Thank you for being a good friend."

"No problem, but you can do better than a guy who can't be around even if he has tons of money." I hug her, but his money has nothing to do with why I love him.

CHAPTER FIVE

WILL

I'VE MISSED THE FUCK OUT OF MY FUTURE WIFE, BUT I CONSOLE myself with the fact that soon she'll be mine. It's been six months since I've seen her, and the torture is unbearable. The only thing that has helped me through it is the knowledge that she loves me the way I love her.

It's been difficult to keep my distance, but it's for the best because I want to flip her over my shoulder and fill her with every inch of me until she understands we're one forever. We'd crossed the line within seconds in each other's presence, and now that I've had a taste of her, the need to feel her is agonizing.

Still, at Christmas, I sent her a giant gift and had her guard deliver it to the door while I watched from the safety of my vehicle because I couldn't risk that she answered the door. The stuffed bear was meant to be a replacement for me while she slept at night. Around the neck was a necklace with a book charm because my Melanie is a bookworm and a future librarian. The angry voicemail she sent me made me smile when she realized the necklace wouldn't come off. It has a tracker to keep her safe while I'm gone. Yes, she has guards most of the time, but that doesn't mean shit can't happen, especially when word gets out that she belongs to me.

Her birthday is coming soon, and that's when I'll ask her to marry me and show her our house. I only need to finish the final touches, which seems to take forever. Every time I get close to finishing, something goes wrong. Uncle Jackson came over and had his inspector come over to inform me that the contractor screwed up the entire electricity in one room, forcing me to tear it apart and rebuild the room and the surrounding hallway. Unable to trust anyone else with my wife's future home, I took over the project with the help of my cousins, which meant that I couldn't even steal moments with Melanie. I've been working double time since I returned from school. It's been two damn weeks straight of nonstop work from sunup to sundown.

MY WORK IS FINALLY DONE, AND TODAY IS THE BIG DAY. THE day I've waited for—for so damn long that I could weep—but I've never been one for tears, even when I was a boy. Today I claim my woman. The past three weeks have been grueling, a test of endurance, patience, and heartache as I stayed away from her a little longer than I wanted to, but things had to be just right, and she hadn't been eighteen. If

I'd even heard her voice I would have cracked, given in to the desire that I've held onto for the past four years. My father always said the best things in life required the most sacrifice, and she was the best there could be.

After a long, cool shower, I wash all the grime off me, but I need a haircut and shave. You'd think I've been living in the wilderness instead of the edge of Steeleville, working on our future home. Before the haircut, I need to see my father to straighten some things out. Security opens the gate the moment my SUV pulls up. I give them a nod, getting a strange look from Damon. I can't read it. The expression is a mix of fear and pride. I don't like or trust it.

I enter the clubhouse courtyard where my father is working on his bike. "Pops, we need to talk." It's a Texas-hot day, but he doesn't bother working in the shade. If I didn't know better, I'd think he had a death wish.

He stands up, stretching out his long, broad frame and then dusts off his hands, giving me a wide smile. "Hey, boy, it's good to see you. How are you doing?"

"Don't you need a water or something, Pops?"

"I could go for a beer, but let's go grab a water because I'm waiting for that gorgeous mother of yours to get her booty over here soon." He grins like he's won a prize. They make being in love a freaking breeze. In all the years they've been married, I'd only heard them argue a dozen times, but they weren't even real arguments, and they were about each other's safety.

We enter the clubhouse, and he pulls two waters from the cooler behind the bar, tossing me one.

I twist open the bottle and take a long drink before setting the drink down on the bar.

"So—you going to tell me what's going on?"

I raise my brows, rubbing my hands together. "It's about that time." Today's the annual Steele barbeque, and I'm going to see her for the first time. We can finally have that talk before we celebrate her birthday tomorrow.

"So you're going to make your move tomorrow?" my father asks.

"Damn right, I am. There's less than a day of waiting left, but there's also something I want to talk to you about."

My father frowns, a sigh falling from his lips. "You're not ready to take over, are you?"

"Pops, I was born ready. I don't know why you ever thought I wasn't planning to take over. Every single one of the guys follows my lead, and I join in everything we do."

"I just figured with college and your past that maybe you had bigger plans."

"Pops, what bigger plans? Steeleville is its own entity. The Riders are important to all of us, to the town, to all our families and friends, and to the safety of everyone around. It's Who. We. Are. I'd like nothing more, and my degree only adds to everything you've built."

He smiles at me, dusting off his hands again on his pants before pulling me into his arms. "Damn, boy, you're going to make me cry. Don't tell your mother," he says, choking up a little.

"Too late," my mother says, coming from the clubhouse doorway with a smirk on her face aimed directly at my father. She turns to me and says, "How are you, my son?" My mother has always had a soft spot for me as her oldest baby boy. Even when I fuck up, she's on my side, guiding me to fix everything.

"I'm good, Mother." It's not quite the truth, but what can I tell her? Honesty won't help the situation.

"You look handsome," she says, pulling me in for a hug and brushing the top of my hair that is way too damn long. "Although, you need to stop running your hands through your hair."

"Yeah, I can't help it." I miss the fuck out of Melanie, and it has been brutal avoiding her. Every time I think of Melanie, I want to break every speed limit to get to her. The temptation is excruciating.

"Well, don't pull your hair out or you'll go bald, and I don't think Melanie would like that very much." She smiles and pats my cheek. I'd gladly go bald if it was Lanie pulling my hair while screaming my name as she rode my cock. The thought makes my balls ache, which isn't smart in front of my mother.

"Well, I'll see you both later. I still have to prepare for the big day tomorrow."

"Good luck, Son. Let us know if you need any help with Beast. He's not going to be pleased with his baby girl getting a boyfriend."

"More like a husband." My parents' eyes widen, and a smirk spreads across my father's face. He shakes his head and pulls my mother into his arms.

"I wish you the best, Son, and I have your back."

"Thanks." I hop into my SUV and drive off. There is a lot to do, including getting a new haircut for today. My beard has gotten a little scruffy and so long that I could almost be mistaken for my father if it wasn't for the color and my lack of tats. Pulling up to the only haircutting spot in town, I don't see Max's pickup in the lot. Fuck, please don't tell me he's not here today. I can't look like shit before I see Melanie. We haven't seen each other in months.

When I park and hop out, Connor smiles as he steps from the same door I'm about to head in. "What's up, cousin?"

"Nothing. Is Max in there?"

"No. Only Chrissy is cutting today."

"Fuck."

"Come on. Relax. She's pretty damn good at it."

"Is that why you're grinning from ear to ear?"

"Nope. Why do you look like shit today? Is it because Melanie's gotten accepted to UNT?"

My mouth falls open, and all thoughts of a haircut slip from my mind. "What the fuck do you mean she got accepted to UNT—which UNT?"

"I don't know. That's what my mom said this morning." There's a huge difference between the one in College

Station and the one in Dallas. Either way, both are from here, but I'd move to Dallas for her. Fuck. My head is pounding in my skull right now. "Before you go losing your shit, you should get cleaned up. Why do you look like shit, anyway?"

"I've been getting our house ready."

"Wow, do you think talking to her before this would have helped?" He has a point, but I thought I made myself clear at Christmas when I let her know that I was serious and that I couldn't just give in. Didn't her father tell her that I had to stay away?

"Shut the fuck up. I told her what it was last year, and at Christmas. Everyone knows I'm a man of my word."

"Well, then, you better figure out what is going to happen because she has other plans that don't involve Steeleville and William Steele." Even though he's not wrong, I want to cold-cock my cousin in the face.

"You're right. I'll fix this, but first, I have to look presentable." I push past him and enter the hair salon. "Chrissy, I'm next."

"The chair's waiting, Prez." I climb into the small salon chair that makes me feel like it's going to break, so I stretch out my long legs. I close my eyes, trying to figure out how I'm going to fix this with Melanie. There's no way I can let her leave me. Yes, she can go to college and do shit, but we're in this together.

"So, what do you need?" Chrissy asks, standing in front of me. I can feel she's a little too close, but I suppose that's how haircuts work. Normally I have Max do it, and he's close, but he's a guy and I don't give a fuck that he's standing in my personal space. However, Chrissy's chest is practically in my face. Somehow that shit doesn't seem right. I tilt my head and move up to give myself a bit of space.

"I want to look clean cut. Presentable."

"For what? You're hot just the way you are. Rugged, sexy as hell. This scruff and the long look would have any girl ready to be the next first lady around here," she purrs, rubbing my face while her breasts are nearly kissing my throat.

"Just do it without the flirting. My dick belongs to someone else, Chrissy. Always has, always will." I remove her hand from my face, doing my best to keep myself under control. My temper is already on edge. She backs up and finally gets to work. After that, she finishes my haircut and shave without any more flirting, which earns her a proper tip. I leave looking like the gentleman that I hope wins Melanie over—if that's what she's looking for because if not, I'll have to fucking kidnap her sexy ass and tie her to my bed until she realizes that we're meant to be together. Last year, she was worried I wouldn't be hers by the time I came back. Now that I'm here, there's no way in hell I'm letting her escape. I've waited too long for her to run scared.

It's fine. There's more than one reason I gave her that charm. It came with a tracker. She can try to run, but I'll always know where to find my bride.

CHAPTER SIX

MELANIE

TOMORROW I TURN EIGHTEEN, AND I'M SO EXCITED FOR IT. I'M hoping that's why Will has ghosted me these past few weeks since he graduated, or has he changed his mind? We haven't had more than a handful of texts after our kiss. I wished him a happy graduation, but all he said was thank you. Since then, all my messages have been left unread. Beth wanted to take a stroll through town before I had to work and we did a quick bit of shopping at the bookstore and grabbed a cup of coffee. It's going to be a long day, but all I want to do is see him again.

I finish my coffee cup and stop to toss it in the trash can. "We really need to go into Dallas and hit up a real club," Beth says, tossing the rest of her croissant and drink.

"Yeah, like my dad would let me," I reminded her. She's met him so many times already so she should know better.

She nudges my elbow. "He will when you go off to college."

"He wouldn't *let* me." My dad has always taken my safety and that of my family's extremely seriously so there's no way he wouldn't freak out if I was out clubbing so far away from Steeleville where he couldn't be close enough to rescue me if necessary.

"No, but what he doesn't know won't hurt him."

"Somehow, I'm sure he'd know." If one of my siblings doesn't have tabs on me, one of the prospects is looking out for my safety. Honestly, having heard horror stories from the past, I don't mind being protected, but I do wonder what it would be like to let loose every once in a while.

"What's it like having such nosy parents?" Beth's family abandoned her a long time ago. They don't give a shit what she does and she doesn't either. My parents don't care for the freedom she has or her influence on me, but they trust my judgement.

"I love them even if it's sometimes suffocating." I roll my eyes and keep moving down the street. My heart nearly bursts from my chest when I spot a familiar vehicle.

"Isn't that Will's SUV?" my bestie, Beth, says. I do my best to feign ignorance.

"Is that his ride?" I question, squinting my eyes even though my vision is perfect and the sun is behind us. I miss him, but he's been back for almost three whole weeks and hasn't bothered to see me. Not once has he come to the house to stop by, and he's ignored my messages.

I already know he has a no-call policy because he needed to focus on school and I was a sensual distraction. I understood it because there were nights when my body wouldn't sleep when I thought of his voice saying my name with such lust. It still drives me insane.

She nudges me with her shoulder, smirking. "Please. We've known him for years. Of course it is—look at the plates."

"Whatever. So he's back in town. Big deal. I wonder how long he's been here because he hasn't visited me, and he graduated three weeks ago." I hold my head up high because that's what I was taught.

"Well, that's why they're having a barbeque—to celebrate his graduation. He must be getting a haircut to look good for someone." She bumps me with her elbow.

"Whatever," I answer with a blush on my face. When we pass by the shop window, we sneakily steal a peek. He's there, all right. The man I've had a crush on since I was like thirteen. The man who promised me the world and his fidelity while telling me to be a good girl has Chrissy and her ample breasts in his face, getting a full view and loving the show. She's holding his face, and then he closes his eyes and holds her hand. I swallow hard, attempting to control the bile rising in my throat.

"That bitch has her hands on your man."

With all my strength, I keep my tone level. "He was never mine and never will be. He's obviously enjoying his time with the local doorknob."

"Damn, girl. Let it out," she says with a giggle.

I turn and glare at her. "I'm starting to think you like my misery."

She hugs me. "Come on girl, you know I love you, but I'm tired of seeing you mope around for a man that hasn't been around just because he told you to stay put like a damn dog. I like that fire."

"It's cool. I guess I should stop turning guys down then."

"Yeah, especially Damon, who can't keep his eyes off you." Her head tilts upward, and I realize that Damon isn't more than fifteen feet ahead. He must be on my babysitting duty this morning. Beth drags us past the salon and right in front of Will's large, sleek SUV. I wonder if he fucks that whore in there. My chest aches, thinking about it.

"Good morning, Damon," Beth says, tossing him a wink. "So Mel could use a date." My mouth falls open, shocked that she's so damn bold. I'm sure my face is comically red.

"I'm available on Tuesday," he says, smiling at me with all that charm he brings every time I see him. Except every time he's watched over me, I've made it clear that I'm not up for dating.

"What a coincidence—so is Mel," Beth cheers. I want to kick her and say I can't, but then I see my reflection in Will's SUV, and I don't deny her interference.

"Well, it sounds like a date," Damon says. "I'll see you then." Beth takes my arm and leads me away before I can change my mind and tell him I'm not available for dating. Great. He's going to think I like him more than I do. He's handsome and buff, but my fragile heart isn't interested in dating even though I'm suffering.

"That's what I'm talking about. Well, how about we go pick a dress? Do you want to bring him to the barbeque?" Beth wags her brows up and down, grinning like a fool.

I look back at the salon, feeling like my chest is about to explode. "Do you think he's going to bring Chrissy?" My voice shakes and gives me away. She doesn't need to ask who because there's only one person I could be talking about.

Beth grips my shoulders and hugs me. "No way. He'd be stupid to do that. She's bedded like half the guys in town. It would be stupid to think that he'd be proud to bring her around his mother." Yes. Mrs. Steele doesn't like Chrissy at all. She gets her hair done by Maria, the other female stylist in town.

As we walk back to my car, I fight back the tears. My phone buzzes and it's my mother, reminding me about the barbeque today and that I promised to help Penny at the bakery. "I have to go to the bakery so that everything is ready for today."

"I can go with you."

"You don't have to. We still have to get dressed, and you take a lot longer than me."

"Fine, but I'll see you later, and remember—you have a date with Damon on Tuesday. That asshole can tag you, but it's nothing but a pretty book. We can drive to Dallas and have it removed whenever you want," she says.

"Yes, we can. That's a great idea, and I should have done it two weeks ago."

"That's my girl." She smacks my ass before giggling and hopping in. I walk around the front and make my way to her place, dropping her off first before hitting the bakery.

By the time I arrive, I've swallowed back the pain of this morning and I'm able to focus on my job. Okay, focus isn't what I call it, it's more about compartmentalizing my feelings. It's how I've managed to get through the past year without Will. Putting my heart in a little box and hiding it away, so it doesn't break. Now that it's cracked in half, I need it there, locked away so I don't shatter to pieces.

"There's my favorite assistant. I'm so surprised you don't want to be a baker because you're so good at it." I can smell the bullshit from the front door. I love Aunt Penny like everyone else, but I'm one of the few who offered to help.

"I'm hardly your favorite. You have Daisy, of course, and let's not forget all of your other children. I'm just the one you conned into working today."

"You got me there, but you're one of my favorites." She gives me a squeeze and then hooks her arm over my shoulder and walks me into the back. "You're special, little Melanie. Come on, and let's get this done before my husband comes hunting me down." She laughs, and we get to baking for the next two hours.

I make it through the work at the bakery with the many treats for the celebration, including a large cake for Will. All the while, I fight the urge to vomit from the reminder of him and his special day. A celebration I thought I would be a big part of. Jackson comes in with a big grin, "Hello ladies, are you ready to take this stuff over there?" He gives his wife a huge smile.

"Give us a minute. The cake is ready, but it's massive."

"I'll take it, beautiful. I don't want our nephew's cake ruined. Crystal will have my ass." We laugh because she'll tear him a new one. He pushes the cart out to his truck and then comes back in to get another stack of trays.

Penny walks up to me with a big smile and says, "You can go. We got the rest from here. Thank you so much for today. I can't wait to see you later." She hugs me and then I go in the back to take off my apron and get my things. Once I hit the outdoor air, I feel the Texas heat hit me and it's almost as bad as working in the bakery kitchen all morning.

My phone rings just as I hit the remote start. I stand outside the car and pull it out of my pocket to see it's Damon's calling. It takes me a second while I debate if I should answer it and on the last ring, I do. "Hey, I'm just leaving the bakery. What's going on?"

"I'm heading over to the barbeque today. Will I see you there?" he asks, sounding nervous, anxious. Nothing like the guy I've spoken to almost four times a week. Why is he acting shy? Does he really have feelings for me?

"You're going?" I question, panic setting in. Honestly, I'm not ready to start dating even though I'm so done with Will.

"Yes. I'm one of the guards for the day." I release a cool breath of relief. "Will I be seeing your cute face there?"

"Yes, of course. My father is a Rider," I reminded him.

"Great. Are we on for Tuesday?"

"Um...I'm not sure if that's a good idea." As I say that, I see none other than Chrissy passing me on the street. I'd love to run her over with my car. "You know what? Yes, I'll go."

"Good. See you later, beautiful."

I end the call, and although Damon is cute and fun to talk to, I'm not interested in him. I shouldn't lead him on when my heart belongs to a man I can't be with. William Steele broke all my trust today. I've waited for him, and he's proven to be full of shit.

I drive home to clean up for a party that I no longer want to attend. Just as I pulled up, I saw my father's vehicle still in the driveway. Damn it, my parents are still there. Unable to waste more time, I rush into the house because the party has already started.

"Hey, sweetie. Do you want us to wait for you?" my father calls out as I rush up the stairs to my bedroom.

I have a feeling I'm going to be an emotional wreck, so I won't be able to drive. "Yes. I'll only be a few minutes."

"Okay."

I close my bathroom door and quickly tug off my tee shirt, tossing it into my laundry basket. Goodness, I need a shower, so I jump in for a fast rinse off and scrub down without doing my hair. I suppose it's better than being a sweaty, sugary mess.

I'm down in ten with my hair in a cute ponytail and wearing a pair of tiny khaki green shorts and a cut-off shirt that shows my flat abs. My dad growls. "Are you trying to have Will and me kill some of the boys there?"

"Come on, Dad. I'm about to be eighteen and as far as I'm concerned there's nothing going on between Will and I, so I'm single. Although I do have a date coming up with Damon."

"I thought you had something going on with Will," my mother adds in confusion. I shake my head, unable to discuss it without feeling my throat close up. My parents stare at me in confusion. Pressing my lips together, I don't speak for at least thirty seconds.

My father says, "Is something going on between the two of you?" His gaze is laced with suspicion.

"No, he is taking me to the movies on Tuesday. It's not that big of a deal."

My father's face shifts into a menacing smirk, and my mother and I stare at him before he says, "I don't like it."

"It's not like anything's going to happen, and I'm not going to marry the dude. I'm about to head off to college and I haven't been on a proper date, and obviously someone else forgot I existed."

My father shakes his head, wrapping his arm around my mother's shoulder. "I suppose you're right. I just don't want you falling head over heels with anyone and forgetting about your dreams."

Too late. Dreams are shattered.

My mother looks at me under my father's arm with a sympathetic smile, understanding my plight. She watched me waiting by the window for weeks after Will returned home from college without a single visit or call. Three fucking weeks, and not a word.

"Fine. We need to go, but I'm telling you I don't think it's a wise move, Princess."

"You don't want anyone dating me," I huff and walk out the front door, refusing to listen to his naysaying.

A minute later, they're both hopping into the SUV with my other brother, who's scowling at me and shaking his head. I roll my eyes at him because I'm not in the mood for anyone's nonsense. I've been on the verge of tears all day, and they wouldn't understand. They have no idea that Will broke my heart, and I can't tell my father because a war would break out if he knew.

We drive to the clubhouse and as we pass the gate, my father gives Damon a once-over. He crooks his finger, summons him over, and then whispers something to him. The second we drive past them and into the parking spot, I ask, "What did you say?"

"I just gave him a warning, Princess."

"Daddy," I hiss.

"What? You're my little girl, and I'm not going to let any fucking dick play with you. If he's too weak to take you out, then it's his problem. Damon knew who you were before he asked you out, right?"

"Yes, of course. You assigned him to my guard duty."

"Well, then?" I don't like the tone in his voice. My father's a district attorney, which means he's slick as hell with skills to play mind games easily.

"Okay."

"Good. Now, let's have some fun. I hope I get some of those brownies you made."

"Not if the kids get them first," I say, knowing they're a hit with everyone and will be gone as soon as the smell spreads across the yard.

"They'll have to fight me for them," he says. He unlocks the vehicle and we all start getting out. I hope I can avoid running into Will for as long as possible.

As soon as we pop out of the vehicle, I spot Will, and he stops talking to his father. His eyes land on me, and his face goes from a smile to a hardened stare. I ignore him and walk off in the opposite direction toward my friends who are huddled together, but I don't make it far when I feel Will's presence on my heels. It's almost as if he's breathing down my neck. Speaking of neck, my locket is hot against my breasts. If I could tear this necklace away from my neck, I would. Maybe my father could have it removed if I ask.

CHAPTER SEVEN

WILL

"Mel, what the hell are you wearing?" I bark out, pulling her inside the clubhouse hallway away from everyone. We haven't seen each other in months, and this isn't how I wanted our reunion to go. I had a few hours left before I could officially make her mine. Today is going to be torture, and I don't need this.

"Excuse me. My name is Melanie, Mr. Steele. Please do not address me again." She storms away from me, and I'm about to fucking lose my mind. Did I miss something?

"Since when did we become so damn formal with each other?" I snarl, wanting to bend her over my knee and see how quickly she forgets formalities. Damn it, I want to forget all the rules and just take her now. *A few more hours.*

"Again, you're speaking to me and I'm not sure why. I don't know who you are anymore. You must be mistaking me with someone else because I can't be the same woman you made all those promises to. You led me to believe there was more. Now, please get the hell out of my face because I don't want to see your stupid, lying face anymore."

"Why? What did I do?"

"What did you do?" She laughs in my face. "I can't believe you. Three fucking weeks, Mr. Steele. You've been in this small motherfucking town for three whole weeks, and you couldn't even be bothered to speak to me, call me, or even acknowledge me when you came back. Then I see you give other women your attention just fine. So do me a favor—let's keep it that way. I'm leaving in just under two months, and I won't see you for a long time." I'm struck dumb by the notion that she's really going away to college in August.

Like a fool, I take too long to respond, so she continues with added venom. "Hopefully it will be a very long time, and then *maybe* we'll both be married to other people by then."

She sets me off with those words because there is no way another man will ever have his hands on her. I have her pinned to the island. "You're not marrying anyone else."

"No, you'll just be fucking them, but I'm sure as hell not ever marrying you. Goodbye, William Steele. Congrats on graduating to being a heartbreaker." She pushes my chest and moves under my arm, storming off.

"Lanie, wait," I shout, rushing to the clubhouse door, but her bestie Beth gets in the way just in time for me to lose sight of her in the crowd. "So, future Prez, isn't it weird to have sex with the same woman as everyone else?"

"My sex life is none of your business."

"It is when it upsets my best friend after she's spent the last year waiting for your selfish ass," she snaps, getting all up in my face. I'd shove her out of the way, but I was raised with manners, and I also need to understand what the hell she's going on about. If there's anyone who knows what's running around in Melanie's mind, it's Beth.

"I don't know what the fuck you're talking about," I snarl. "So, you better explain or get the fuck out of my way before I move you."

Her eyes turn to slits and then she lets it all out. "Chrissy. We saw you today, and you looked awfully cozy in that chair with your hands on her, and her tits couldn't be any closer to your face unless they were in your mouth."

I slam my eyes shut, ready to send my fist into a wall. "It's not what it looked like."

She scoffs, "Isn't that what they all say?"

God, if she was a man, I'd pop her in the mouth. Where the fuck is Connor when I need to punch someone? I don't have time for that kind of ridiculousness. "I don't need to explain anything to you."

"No, but she's my best friend, and she saw the same thing. I had to watch her heart break in front of me because you're whoring around town like she wouldn't find out about it."

Shit. She has it all wrong, and I'm going to destroy Chrissy now. "Where is she? I need to find her."

"How would I know, jackass? I was interrogating you and giving her the space she needed to get away from you," she huffs. Damn sneaky bitch. I knew I didn't like her.

I move past her and search the yard, but I don't see Melanie in that tiny outfit that was made to make me jealous and hard. My angry rave is nowhere to be found.

Taking a calming breath, I come up with a smarter plan to find her. I open up the security cameras on my phone and follow Melanie from the moment she leaves the clubhouse through the yard to the front gate. She's outside with Damon. He's got his hand on her arm. I'm going to fucking break his filthy hand. He knows better than to touch her. All the Riders and the prospects are well aware that she's mine.

I storm through the damn door of the gate. "Get your hands off her right now before I end your life." He's lucky I'm feeling generous enough to give a warning.

"What's wrong, Prez?" Damon backs up right away, but it isn't enough for me. His hands were on her, and that's a line he shouldn't have crossed. I haven't forgotten the look in his eyes when I came in this morning or the comments that he made last year. He'd kept his behavior on the up and up, but I also never thought about him again after Christmas break because I had secured my woman. How fucking foolish of me.

"What's wrong is you have your hands on my woman," I snarl, moving closer to him, losing all sense of control.

"I don't belong to you," Melanie says as if she really believes it.

"The fuck you don't, Melanie. I thought we went through this last year." I've had enough of this talk. She's the only non-family member that's ever been on my bike and the only woman who will ever ride my dick, so she needs to quit this little fit and we need to talk.

My father comes to the front with Beast following close behind. "What the hell is going on out here?" Beast snaps. He already knows how I feel and where I stand. Hell, last week he even pitched in to finish the house because it meant the world to me to have it done on time for tomorrow.

"Your daughter is being difficult," I grumble, although a part of me understands I'm being unreasonable. Another part of me is feeling murderous, and that gaze lands on Damon's bitch ass.

"Will, is there something you haven't told me?" Beast snarls, chest and nose flaring.

"That your daughter is about to get this fuck killed."

He scoffs and then tips his chin. "Good. I've already told him to stay away from her." I'm glad we see eye to eye because if he even dared to give this asshole any leeway, I'd lose it. He's supposed to back me up on this.

"What?" Melanie shouts, staring at her father in shock.

"Sweetheart, as a prospect, he knows that you and Will are a couple, but then he pulls some shit like asking you out." I'm on Damon in a heartbeat as the last words leave DA

Brandon's mouth. My hand is around his throat, lifting him off the ground as I watch the color drain from his face.

"You what?" I snarl through my clenched teeth. He can't get a word out because I'm cutting off his air supply. He dared to hit on my future wife, ask her out, and try to take her away from me. He must want to die or be the stupidest motherfucker on the planet.

"Please let Damon go," she screams, tugging on my arm.

As good as it should feel to have her touch me, the sound of his name coming from her lips feels like a betrayal. "No. You were going to date this piece of shit. Now I want him dead even more."

My father grips my shoulder. "Come on, now. Let him go, Son. He's done with the Riders. He betrayed his brothers; he betrayed the future president of the Riders." I let him fall into a heap on the ground, ripping the prospect patch from his vest and kicking him in the balls.

"Daddy, take me home please," I hear her say through the blood rushing in my ears.

"Sure, sweetheart." He pulls her into his arms, and she refuses to look at me. My chest burns so painfully with anger that I storm through the gate, passing everyone at the party to get into the clubhouse, needing to get away from her before I say or do something I regret.

I'm grateful there's a gym on the second floor because my temper needs an outlet. My first hit to the punching bag nearly sent it off the hooks, but by the fourth shot, I demolished it. That bit of steam seems to cool me off enough to be around people again and not hunt down that piece of shit Damon.

When I come out, she's gone and the men have long sent Damon from the clubhouse and soon, he'll be run out of town. Although the party is partially for me, I don't feel like celebrating. I need to go for a ride. I wish I'd brought my damn bike. My father and cousin Connor are the first to meet me and my dad presses his hand to my chest. "I need to go for a ride."

"Are you sober enough?" my pops asks, staring into my eyes, reading them.

"Of course. I wouldn't dare jeopardize my life just because I'm pissed off."

"Another reason to cool down," my cousin adds. He's way more levelheaded than me, but that's because he's no obsessed yet.

"That's why I want to ride."

"Don't go doing anything stupid."

"I'm not. If I stay here any longer, I might hunt that fucker down and kill him. Does anyone else know how long he's been after my woman?" I question, looking at my father who has several of the elder Riders around him. They are all like uncles to me and have taught me so much, but right now, my guts are tied in knots and I want to fight someone.

"No. I doubt he would have made his plans known to any of us."

"Beast fucking knew," I say.

"Yeah, and he shut that shit down."

"True, but that doesn't mean much because he didn't tell me anything." My father's phone rings a moment later.

"What's going on, Beast?" He listens to whatever Melanie's father says and then ends the call. "So, it seems your woman saw Chrissy clinging all over you at the salon and then ran into Damon and agreed to a date out of hurt."

I nod. "Yeah, that's kind of what Beth said without mentioning the date," I say, biting back my anger. She left that key fucking detail out, but I'm sure that was intentional.

"Beast showed her the footage from inside the salon."

"There are cameras inside the salon?" I

"Yeah. You remember when your mother went in there and there were some fuckers flirting with her and they dared to touch her?" I growled, remembering the fuckers that had the nerve to put their hands on her.

"Max kicked them out and the fucker dared to challenge him, but those fools had no idea that Law wouldn't call you."

"Yes, and I was on them in a heartbeat, ready to bash their heads in for trying to intimidate my wife." I chuckled because my father wasn't the kind of man who allowed anyone to mess with his wife.

And I was just like him. Thinking about Damon putting his hands on Melanie riled me up again. "I need to get out of here for a bit."

"Take my bike. It's just been retreaded and tuned up," my pops says.

"Okay. I'll be back in just an hour."

"Give her time," a soft voice comes from the doorway, and it's Melanie's mother. "She loves you, so whatever happened, I'm sure it will work itself out." I press my lips together, nod and leave, needing to clear my head.

Strolling out to the back of the yard where the bikes are set up, I grab my father's and climb on. I need an hour or so to clear my mind and get the tension to roll off my neck. Every muscle in my body is tight and ready for war. Speeding around toward the front and away from the party, I head toward the gate where the prospects monitoring it open it up.

The wind hits my face as I speed through Steeleville, and I decide to ride around the perimeter instead of driving through town. There's just no way I want to run into anyone. The one thing I do is avoid driving past the Brandon home because I'll be tempted to tear down that door and claim my woman, giving no fucks about the problems between us or the hours before she turns eighteen.

I'm a little more than an hour into my ride before I get my temper under control. Once I ride into the Riders yard, the party is fully underway and everyone is cheering when they see me. Several of my cousins are waiting for me as I park my father's bike, but first my father stops me and pulls me aside.

He grips my shoulders and stares deep into my eyes. "Are you good?"

"Yeah. I calmed down, but I can't wait until the morning."

"Just have some fun here. Then you'll see your future wife, and everything will be okay."

"Thanks, Pops." We head into the crowd where my cousins surround me and hand me a drink.

"Congrats, Cousin. You're the first of us to finish college, and now you're about to take the lead in your father's business," my cousin Daisy says. "Too bad you screwed it up with Mel."

"Don't worry. I'm going to fix that tomorrow, and she'll be your cousin soon," I insist, taking a drink of my beer while staring off into the distance and thinking of the future with my wife. Melanie and I will have our happily ever after, and no one will get in the way—no one.

CHAPTER EIGHT

MELANIE

I COULDN'T GET AWAY FROM THE PARTY FAST ENOUGH. Watching Will lose control like that had multiple effects on me all at once. A part of me was torn between anger, fear, and lust. He'd gone wild on Damon for asking me out, even though he was cheating on me. It made no sense, but then again, some men thought they were allowed to cheat while their women were forced to take it and be faithful. That isn't me. I'm not going to be the fool.

"Melanie."

"I don't want to talk."

I stare out the window the entire car ride to the house, refusing to look at my father. He calls my mother to inform her that he was taking me home and would be returning quickly. "I won't be long."

"Are you sure you don't want us to come home?" she asks, and I feel like a jerk for ruining their time out.

I shake my head, and he answers, "No. Melanie needs time alone."

We pull up to the house and I enter the code, unlocking the front door. I thought I was going to be alone, but my dad followed me into the house, walking past me.

"Dad, what kind of game are you playing at?" I ask as I stomp inside, slamming the front door.

"What kind of game?" he says, feigning ignorance. A professional tactic, I believe.

"You lied to me about your talk with Damon when you really told Damon to back off."

"Princess, you have been in love with Will for a long time, and although I'm a father and not particularly happy about it being so soon, I won't stop you two. I didn't lie about what I said. I just said I warned him off. Damon knows that Will's in love with you and wants you to be his wife, which means not a damn one of the Riders should think twice about approaching you."

"So Will can fuck around, but I can't date anyone?" I hiss, slamming my close-fisted hands down at my sides.

He waves a finger at me. "Young lady, your mouth. And what makes you think he's fucking around?" His brow raises and a muscle in his jaw flexes, telling me my dad's pissed. You wouldn't be able to know it, but I can read my father.

"I saw him with Chrissy at the salon." My voice cracks when I let the words fall from my lips, and I see my father fall into full protective daddy mode. He wraps his arms around me, holding me as I fall apart. He loosens his grip briefly, and I can tell he's texting.

"Just letting your mother know I'll need a little longer."

"It's okay. I'll be fine."

"No, you won't. At least not until we get this situation straightened out, because I never want my little princess feeling any kind of pain." He kisses my temple. "Chrissy? You think that he'd waste his time with her? Sweetheart." I can't fight the tears flowing down my face. "Would you feel better if I showed you something?"

"What?" He takes my hand and leads me to his office, pulling out a chair from in front of his desk and bringing it around beside his chair. "Take a seat for a minute."

He takes a seat in his leather chair and then turns on his computer. I watch him log into several password-encrypted links before it finally opens up to a set of security cameras. "We're in the town's main cameras. Many of the shops have their own cameras, and we have access to all of them for safety reasons. The salon is no different. Now—when was this encounter?"

"Earlier today, around nine." He nods. When he loads the screen, I see inside the salon and there is the image before me. Will is standing way off, too close to the door. Almost afraid to enter. She moves toward him like a hunter stalking her prey. I can't make out what she says to him, but then he takes a seat closer to the camera, and my father turns up the sound. Every word uttered from her filthy mouth nearly makes me vomit, but Will's reaction changes everything. He's angry and possessive of me.

"What have I done?" I gasp.

"Sweetheart, if you only saw a part of this… Hell, when I saw part of this, I wanted to rip his head off. Chrissy has a bad habit of taking men with weak minds. Will isn't the kind, especially after all this time." He's always had a soft spot for Will. I don't know if it's because they have the same name, which bothers me a bit, or because he's close with Boomer, but either way, he's not wrong. Will hadn't betrayed me. In fact, he'd only proven his devotion to us.

Before my father leaves, he tells me to give it time. I'm sure about what I need to do. My heart aches in a way that I don't understand. I've loved William Steele for years, letting my heart hope he'd be true. It was so hard, and yet I've failed him by accepting a date because I felt abandoned and betrayed.

I stay in my bedroom for the rest of the day, wanting to avoid all conversation about the incident or anything to do with Will and just hide. My mother brings some food up to my room, and although my stomach is doing somersaults, I manage to eat a little. Unable to sleep, I take a long shower, crying my heart out.

It isn't until one in the morning that my body finally gives in to the stress and sadness of my own silliness and I pass out. Unfortunately, it doesn't keep me asleep. Nightmares of Will hating me fill my dreams. I lie in bed until the sound of the doorbell startles me out of my thoughts. Scrambling for my phone, I check and it's only seven.

It's probably my bestie coming to surprise me for my birthday. She's like that. We've been friends for the past two years. A soft knock at my bedroom door tells me it's my mother. "Hey, Mom. Come on in."

"What's up?" I ask when she enters. Of course, she looks perfect even though it's only seven in the morning and she's not even dressed for visitors yet. My mother is the epitome of beauty. I wonder how she does it after having all of us kids.

"You have a visitor downstairs." She gives me a sheepish smile.

"Who?"

"Will." My heart climbs its way into my trachea, nearly choking me.

She walks over to the edge of my bed and takes a seat, patting my hair. "You don't have to see him if you don't want."

"I do...it's just..." I bit down on my bottom lip. "I don't understand this. Us...he made me feel so alone...when he was right there. Like I wasn't good enough to see, and then I saw him, and it only dug the knife in deeper. Why is this so hard?"

"Because men are stupid and try to do things the way they think is right. Will had his reasons, as rational as he believed they were. They had merit, but there is something to be said for age. Trust me when I say even your father made me want to strangle him, and I had my doubts when we first met. Talk to him, and just remember that above all, you are still in control, and we will always be there for you."

"Thank you." She pulls me in for a brief moment before standing and taking her leave. I can always count on her to make things better.

I wash my face and change my clothes into something a little more comfortable. Today's going to hit one hundred degrees, so I opt for a pair of shorts, sandals, and a thin tee shirt. When I step out of my room, Will is sitting at the top of the steps. He quickly jumps to his feet, looking nervously at me. His eyes scan over my body. There's a light rumble that comes from his throat, but I'm not sure if it's a good or bad noise. "Um, Melanie, can we talk?"

"Yes. I think it's about time, but let's not do it here." I don't want any of my siblings or my parents to hear.

"Thank you."

Without hesitation, he takes my hand. The pleasurable sensation is indescribable and hits us both as his eyes meet mine. Our eyes lock, and he pulls me close until my chest meets his. "Will," I whisper. It's been so long, and the memories of that day are flooding back.

"We should go," Will chokes out, and then he leads me down the steps.

My parents are sitting in the living room. "We'll be back," I mutter as we continue past them.

"Where are we going?" I ask Will, scrunching my brows as he leads me well past the front of my house.

He smirks a little too slyly for me and says, "Just for a walk."

"I'm hardly dressed for anything special." I'm dressed for almost anything, but I'm trying to gauge his motives.

"I think you look beautiful. Downright sexy, as a matter of fact, birthday girl."

I blush, dipping my head. "Thank you."

He tips my chin, bringing my eyes up to look at him. "Don't thank me. I'm the one blessed to look upon you." He brings my hand to his lips and kisses it, causing my pussy to drool all over my panties like a foolish, pathetic little girl. Why does this man have his hooks in me so deep? Because I've loved him since I was a little girl, even before I knew what love really was.

CHAPTER NINE

WILL

FUNNY HOW I AVOIDED SEEING HER FOR MONTHS, BUT KEEPING my distance for a few hours had been torture. I'd been up since three in the morning, pacing throughout my apartment, trying to figure out what to say. How to make her see that I was in this for life and that no one would ever come between us.

"Um…Lanie. I don't know where to begin."

She tugs her hand from mine and huffs with that cute little sass that drives me wild. She stops in the middle of the sidewalk and crosses her arms under her ample breasts, pushing them upward. That thin top does nothing to hide how fucking hard her nipples are. "You can start with why you abandoned me for the past three weeks. I sent you a 'congratulations' and received a general thanks. Nothing else. All my messages were left unread." Fuck…

"Babe, I don't have the same phone anymore. Graduation morning, I accidentally ran it over. Due to security concerns, I didn't save in a cloud, and my card in the phone was crushed. Because I was busy, I didn't bother getting a new phone for three days. By then, you didn't message me again."

"Why would I have bothered?"

"I wanted to message you, but then I would have kidnapped you, tied you to my bed, and made love to you all night long."

"You make it sound so terrible."

He cups my elbow and pulls me into his arms, cupping my cheek. "Your father would have hunted me down. Besides, I promised my mother that I wouldn't take advantage of you."

"Is that what you were fighting about in the jewelry store?"

"Yes. She already had me make that promise and I'd broken it, so she was angry with me."

"Oh."

"It's been difficult to keep my distance. I promise you that I've never touched another woman or given in to anyone's flirtation or outright offers. I don't know what you think you saw between Chrissy and me, but there was nothing going on."

"I know. My father showed me the footage inside the salon."

"Yeah, I forgot about that until your father called mine to tell us."

"Yes, and I still want to punch her in the face for putting her hands on you and for even cutting your hair."

"Normally Max does it, but I didn't want you to see me looking like a bum, so I gave in. Maybe it's time you learned to cut hair."

"Maybe, I will," she says, tilting her lips.

"Where do we go from here?" she asked.

"Well, I hope we start all over and begin with happily ever after."

"I have a feeling we're going to have lots of bumps in the road."

"As long as you're with me, I'll do all I can to smooth out those bumps. So why have you been so busy? What have you been doing? I know nothing about you."

I sigh because I have no secrets, but there's a lot to tell. "I decided to get multiple degrees, and then I started taking over my father's company little by little. I'm becoming vice president, and eventually I will be the president of the Riders. But for the past few weeks—or rather, months—my true occupation and focus has been this." I stopped her in front of our house that I built.

"This is why you've been busy?" Her wonder and awe are captured in her voice and expression. Fuck, I'm so damn happy she loves it. I slide open the control panel and enter the code, opening the gate.

"Yes, doing this. Some things haven't gone according to plan." Her eyes widen and her lips twist. I take her hand and lead her through the gate, closing it behind us. As safe as I feel in Steeleville, we need our privacy.

"Am I going to fall through the floor?" she asks with a serious face before cracking a grin. The light in her eyes goes straight to my dick, but I have to hold it together so I decide to punish her for being a smart ass.

I pull her in close and my fingers clutch her waist, tickling her sides. "Oh my God, stop. Okay, okay. I quit. I'm sorry," she giggles. Her laughing plea stops me as I hold on to her tightly, breathing in that perfection.

"Hardly a danger of falling through anything, I was talking about delays with delivery dates," I growl against her ear, biting down on her lobe. Fuck, I'm tempted to fill her up on our front lawn.

"Lanie, please tell me you're on birth control."

"I am. My mom recommended it. You don't want babies with me? I thought you'd be like the rest of the men here... like your father."

"My father was much older when he had me. As much as I can't wait to start our family, we have plenty of time for it. Besides—as I recall, you have ambitions that don't include having little ones just yet."

"Rett, I love you."

"Melanie, my love for you will never fade. You're everything to me, and to know you love me has made my existence." I cradle her face with my calloused hands and slide them into her hair, bringing her lips to mine and kissing the lips that I've missed so much. "My world."

She moans as my mouth connects with hers. Our hearts race, and my hunger for her only grows. I bracket my arm around her waist and carry her up the four wooden porch steps. As much as I want to take her inside and fill her womb, it's not time. Walking over to the swing, I sit my future wife in my lap.

She pulls back and tilts her head with a bit of surprise. "Um…we're not going inside?"

"Not yet. I can't be trusted."

"Why? Are you going to deflower this poor, innocent damsel?" She gasps in horror.

"You have no idea. I told you, sweetheart, that the thought of being with you drives me insane. Every day, every hour, every minute away from you is insanely painful. I spent hours upon hours working to distract myself. I'd either be in class, in the gym, or building something to keep myself from thinking about you and wanting to hold you again. Those stolen moments before Christmas were a mistake and a fucking blessing all at once. I got to taste you and know instead of just guessing. They haunted my dreams, filled my fantasies." She squirms in my lap.

"You're not helping," she whines.

"I know. Trust me, I know." My hands hold her still on my thick rod that's painfully hard. If her father pulled up right now, he'd know damn well what was going on. Maybe it would be better to take her into our home.

"How about we tour our home?"

"Our home?"

"Yes, my lovely Melanie—our home. I wouldn't have built this for anyone else."

"I know you said it, but I still find it unfathomable."

"I'm not sure why. Have you met our fathers? It's only natural that we both give the most and accept the best." Her arms wrap around my neck, squeezing tightly as she kisses my chin. "I'm so in love with you, Rett. This can't be real."

"Why are you waiting for the other shoe to drop?" I ask her. We've lived with parents who had spectacular marriages.

"I guess because we've lived a charmed life, and everything can't be this great all the time."

"How was the past year?"

"It was brutal. Sad."

"How was yesterday?"

"One of the worst days of my life."

"Well, then, I'd say not everything is always peaches and cream, sweetheart. We're going to have bad times. Don't worry them into fruition. Let's just live for today. Remember—you're starting college soon, and that means a lot of time away from me."

"I'm still coming home every day."

"And I'll be working long hours, so we'll both be tired and grumpy, which means bad attitudes at times. See…don't worry, because we'll have plenty of strife to keep the pure, unadulterated happiness at bay." She swats my hand.

"You are an ass."

"See? There it is." The giggle is back, and I want to hold her forever. Can a man be this obsessed? Is it even right? It shouldn't be and probably isn't, but ask me if I care because I sure don't. Melanie is my world and my reason for breathing every day.

"Now, come along, Ms. Brandon. It's time I took the birthday girl for a tour of her home so I can remove her clothes and explore her in her birthday suit."

"We don't need a tour for that. Just a little privacy and hopefully a nice soft surface."

"I believe you're trying to kill me."

"Considering how long I've dreamed of this, how many long nights my giant teddy and I snuggled as I imagined he was you, I doubt you're the only one in need."

"Fuck, baby. Tell me about you and your teddy bear."

"Oh, you don't want to know. You'll make me get rid of him."

"No, I won't. Why do you think I bought him, Lanie? I wanted you to rub your sweet little pussy all over it, grinding on it while you thought of me at night. Were you worked up? Needy?"

"Yes. So many nights I went to bed reading books and thinking about what you'd do to me if we were alone. I remembered the way you kissed me. Your hands on my breasts at the store. Your breath on my throat. My pussy was dripping with so much need that I ached for you to make it stop, but you weren't there. Only your gift. The one you demanded I keep to take your place while you were gone."

"Tell me. Did you come on the bear?" She blushes, her rounded cheeks turning a reddish pink. "Answer me, beautiful."

"Yes. Many times." She gasps as my fingers tease her panties. They're soaked, drenched with desire as she recounts the orgasms that I helped her get. Damn. I'm so hard right now, I could come, knowing that she pleasured herself like I hoped she would. I'm almost pissed at myself for not putting a camera in the bear, but that would have been going too damn far. I love her too much to stoop to such an invasion of her privacy.

"I would have loved the show," I grunt. My body aches to fill her with every inch of my cock, but we have to take this slow for both our sakes. I might have rubbed out a thousand times, but that doesn't mean I've got any idea how to last inside her perfect, untouched warmth.

"Where is the bedroom?"

"This way," I take her hand in mine and lead her upstairs to the master bedroom. Her mouth falls open when she sees the double doors. "Yes, I wanted our room to be massive."

"Why? What do you have planned, Mr. Steele?"

"Nothing major, but you need a large closet, and I wanted to include a desk in here as well." I open the room, and she gasps.

"It's stunning."

"That it is," I answer, but my eyes haven't left her perfect face.

"Oh, William Garrett Steele. Take me to bed before I demand you take me standing up."

"Yes, ma'am." I slide my hands under her ass and lift her over to the bed, growling as my fingers feel the soft curves. Fuck, my body has never felt so alive. Having waited for her makes this moment so much better. As I sit her on the edge of the bed, my hands send her tee upward. "You feel so good, Lanie. I'm going to worship you, fuck you, and love you."

"Please. I've missed you, Will. I've longed for you in ways I don't fully understand. Please show me." I push her down, pressing my lips to hers, kissing a path along Melanie's jaw and her throat. I lick a path up and down the column of her neck. Light moans fall from her mouth as the bed depresses from my weight on hers. Sweat forms on my brow as my body heats. I need to get both of us undressed before I lose it.

I stand up and tear my shirt off over my head, tossing it on the floor. Melanie's eyes widen and her mouth parts. "Wow," she gasps, reaching out for me, hooking her hand into my waistband.

"Whoa, gentle. You're going to hurt yourself."

"Big boy, I'm totally fine. I just need you naked."

"Shimmy out of your tiny shorts," I growl, gripping my belt buckle and sliding it through the metal hook and clasp until it comes undone. It clinks, and her attention is once again drawn to my waist. "Eager for me to lose my pants, aren't you?"

"Yes." Her pearly whites grip the edge of her bottom lip. "Rett."

"You're taking too damn long for me," I growl, reaching down and snagging the bottom of her shorts and tugging them off her body. My dick jumps against my boxers as I stare at the wet patch between her thighs.

"You're the one taking too long, Mr. Steele. I can't keep waiting for you." I bend down and slap her pussy.

"You will wait, baby girl. I've waited so damn long for this, years of jerking my cock to thoughts of getting between these slick, slender thighs, hoping to taste this juicy pussy before I stuff you. You're going to be a good girl whether you like it or not because if you misbehave, I'll tie your ass up and take my time licking this tight little hole with my tongue until you pass out."

She whimpers, rolling her hips on the bed, grinding her ass on the mattress. "Damn you, William. No wonder you never texted me."

"Damn right. Every message would start off sweet and would have ended up with how much I wanted to be deep inside you," I promise as I slide both my pants and underwear off, standing in front of the woman I love completely naked. "Now—time to tear these panties off because I'm greedy and I want to eat before I fill you up."

I'm on my knees, parting her thighs. My face brushes against her bare mound, and I breathe her in, feeling a rush of excitement and desire after years of longing. "Damn, baby." I swipe my tongue and growl as the first taste is enough to make me nut. Sweat beads down my back as I drive my tongue into her sweetness.

CHAPTER TEN

MELANIE

I SCREAM AS HIS FINGERS PUSH INTO MY SLIT. EVERY PUMP OF his digits sends more pleasure through me. "Rett," I moan over and over, gripping the expensive, cool sheets. He presses his face harder into my thigh, biting me. My orgasm shoots through my entire body, causing my back to arch and my hips to roll. I shout his name so loudly that I panic, thinking someone will hear me, so I clamp my hand over my mouth.

"Baby girl, don't be quiet. This isn't the place to keep those cries and moans silent. I want to hear you shake the rafters." He crawls up my body until he's completely on top of me, and then, smiling down at me, he presses his length right at my entrance. "Are you ready to give me some more?"

"Yes," I answered greedily, pulling him to me for a kiss. He growls and takes my mouth in a penetrating kiss before pushing the tip inside. My breath is stolen as he slides all the way into me, claiming my virginity. "Oh God," I sigh, unable to move. He freezes, staring into my eyes.

"I'm sorry." He kisses my lips and my cheeks.

"It's fine, Will. I promise. You're just enormously large."

He chuckles and kisses me. "Thank you."

"Thank you," I purr, loving the fullness even though it's practically splitting me in two. My hands cling to his shoulders as he moves slowly in and out until I move with him. Our bodies begin to get wet with sweat as we glide together.

"Fuck, your voice is so damn sexy as hell when you're heated." Does he have any idea how deep his voice is now or how it makes my body vibrate when he speaks?

"You're one to talk, my sexy man." My goodness, the smile on his face is enough to turn me on.

"Babe, I'm doing my best not to come this second. Be a good girl and tell me what you need."

"You're doing a good job like that, Rett. Fuck me." He slams his pretty blues shut and his jaw clenches tight before he begins pumping faster into me. We ride together, but I've asked for more than I can take and more than he can handle.

"Shit, baby girl. Please tell me you're close."

"I'm not, but I don't need to be. I just came. I need you to come and fill me up. God, I need it more than you know,

Rett. I've dreamed about this." He groans, then slows his pace and switches his movements. He rolls his hips, dipping his head and sucking my nipple into his mouth while his fingers slide up and down my hips. Oh God— my pain went completely away and I'm on the edge.

"I'm not giving up, Melanie. My woman isn't going to be satisfied with second best. You always come first. Always." Then his finger slips over my bud, sending me over the precipice.

"I'm coming, Rett. I'm coming again. Holy hell," I shout, scratching down his back until my release comes to an end. Will grips the headboard and roughly pounds into my pussy several more times, coming deep inside of me with a loud roar.

"Fuck, I can't believe it. Wow. Just wow," he sighs, completely out of breath. I wipe the sweat and hair off my forehead and relax as he pulls out and lies beside me on the bed. Will wraps the covers around us and then pulls me on top of his chest. "I've been waiting for this moment for so damn long."

"The sex was amazing."

"I meant this, Lanie. The chance to hold you in my arms." He kisses my forehead, and we lie there in peaceful silence for a long time.

I'm wrapped up in the sheets when his phone rings. "It's your father," he says.

"Oh God." I'm sure all the color drains from my face.

"Relax. I'll answer it, and you get dressed."

"Hello," he says with the coolest, calmest tone, like we didn't just have sex for the first time.

"Where is my daughter?" my father barks over the phone. He's so loud that I can hear him.

"She's right next to me. Why are you yelling?"

"Because I know where you are."

"And? I'm pretty sure you know where we are going to be for the rest of our lives. I thought we discussed this."

"I want to speak to Melanie."

"When you calm down. It's her birthday, and she should be happy. Call back when your temper is regulated." He ends the call, and I gasp.

"I can't believe you just hung up on my dad."

"Melanie, I might have avoided our relationship because I was afraid of this." I pointed to the bed. "But I'm not afraid of taking care of your needs, and that includes your feelings. Today is special, and there is a lot planned for today. I won't let your father's temper get in the way. I hoped that what we just did would have ended our night, but we can't change that now."

"I'm kind of glad it happened now."

"Why?"

"The anticipation is over."

"True. He's calling again."

"Okay. I'll take it." He hands me the phone. "Hi, Daddy."

"Princess, how are you?"

"I'm fine. Will and I spoke. You were right about everything, and although I had my reservations, we made up and I'm happy. He says he has a day planned for my birthday."

Will whispers, "They're included as well."

"He says you're included as well, so I hope you're not upset."

"No, but I don't want to know what you were doing."

"He was showing me our new home."

"New home? So you're ready to move out?"

"Well, didn't you already know about the house?"

"Yes."

"So then you knew I was more than likely willing to move in with him."

"What about getting married?"

"He hasn't asked me."

I turn around, and Will is down on one knee. Damn these men. "Are you two working together?"

"Well, I'm not going to let him shack up with my little girl without a ring."

"Bye, Daddy." I end the call and drop the phone on the desk.

Biting down on my bottom lip, I stare at the love of my life. "Yes, of course." He slides the ring on my finger and then wraps his arms around my waist, spinning me in a circle.

"Put me down, naked man."

"I'm not completely naked."

He does have his pants on, so I suppose he has a point. "This rock is huge."

"That it is, but you deserve it, and I want everyone in town to know you belong to me."

"I'm sure they will. So, are we going to wait to marry?"

"I don't see why. I mean, you can take your time and plan it out with your mom, my mom, and the sisters, but you know, I don't want to wait forever."

"Of course, but we have some time since we don't plan on having any babies any time soon."

"That's right."

"My mom is going to lose it. She's going to want to hit every boutique in Dallas, maybe even New York and Chicago. If we go together, that would work."

"You wouldn't want a girls-only trip? Your dad wouldn't let you ladies go to either of those places unprotected, anyhow."

"Fair point."

"And if anyone is going to protect you, it's going to be me."

"Damn you. Like my panties aren't already a sticky mess. I don't have clothes here. How the hell am I supposed to go home and change?"

"Well, it's a good thing that we're going shopping first. We have a lot to furnish in our home. The bed and the bedspread are the only things I've bought, and my mother helped me with that." My mouth falls open. "Well, she knew damn well I was hanging on by a thread, and she didn't want to make you suffer."

"How am I ever going to look your mother in the face again? It took me forever to do it after the incident at Christmas."

"Oh, honey. Just wait until you accidentally catch my parents walking out of a room together after a few minutes alone. They weren't talking about anything. Let's just say if they could, I'd have another dozen more siblings."

"Oh…"

"Yeah, so don't worry. She'll be blushing before you will. Now, get your pretty ass ready because we have so much to do."

He was right. We only make it back into Steeleville in time to have dinner at Mr. and Mrs. Steele's home where they have it decked out for my birthday. My entire family is here, and the family room has been covered with presents.

"Sweetheart, you look radiant. Now let me see that ring," my mother gushes after giving me a hug. Luckily, we stopped at Will's apartment, a place I'd never been before. I showered and put on a cute pink party dress that cuts off just above the knees. My father scowls at Will all night even though he smiles and hugs me as often as he can, reminding me that I'm his princess.

CHAPTER ELEVEN

WILL

THE FIRST WEEK IN OUR NEW HOME HAS GONE WELL. MOST OF the stuff in my apartment stayed there because my brother moved in, and I only took my clothes, work and school equipment, and photos of Melanie.

Melanie and her mother packed up her room, taking some of her treasures and her clothes. Beast moved it into the house while I was on a job site. The tension between the two of us has grown. Maybe letting his daughter go is harder than he imagined, or the fact that he knows exactly what I'm doing to her every damn night is driving him insane.

Perhaps I shouldn't rub it in his face that I'm hard every time Melanie's name is mentioned, but I'm a twenty-one-year-old man who saved all his firsts for his one and only. He should be happy that I chose his daughter. I could be that backstabbing piece of shit who betrayed the code and tried to steal her from under me.

I work my tail off and come home to find Melanie isn't home yet. I check the tracker, and she's at her parents'. Making the short drive, I rang the doorbell and they let me in. "Hey, Rett. We're in the kitchen."

"Do you want a beer?" Beast asks me. I'm surprised by the peace offering.

"No, thanks." I give Melanie a light peck on the cheek, which causes her to frown.

"What are you making?"

"I'm teaching Mom to make Dad's favorite brownies from scratch. We're on round three."

"Oh. So you're too tired to go out for dinner tonight?"

"A little? I hope you're not upset."

"Not at all. Are all of these bad?" I question, my stomach rumbling. We have some leftovers at home. It's not like we don't have things to eat there, but I promised her a nice dinner together in Dallas.

"Yes," Mary gasps, yanking the plate away.

"Can I have a word with you?" Beast asks.

"Sure." We step into the living room and take a seat.

"I had a talk with Mary today, and she said that Melanie is still going to UNT and that you both aren't planning on any kids any time soon."

"That's the plan."

"So you rushed to get her out of the house because?" Was he really under the impression that I wanted to just knock up Melanie and keep her at home? Yes. I want her to have my babies, but all the Steele Rider wives had careers at one point.

"I've spent my days without her. I love her, and that means giving her what she wants too. If she told me tomorrow that she doesn't want to go and she wants to have babies already, that's what she'd get, but I know she has dreams. We're young. Unlike your generation, Melanie and I were blessed to meet as kids. I didn't need to date to know she was the one. She and I didn't hang out as teens because even then, being around her was painful."

"I'm glad she's not giving up her dreams. I was just worried that these feelings will change in the future." He sighs before taking a long pull from his beer bottle.

I scoff. "I was off at college well before I declared any feelings for her. Never once did any girl draw my notice. Not all the girls in bikinis on the hot days. Trust me when I say my friends were constantly pointing them out and chasing down women. I walked away. My heart and mind always went back to Melanie. I can't explain it because it's not like she's the same girl she was even four years ago. Well, her smile is the same, her laugh is the same, and my need to protect her is the same."

"Good. You remind me of your father, but—"

"Younger and impulsive?"

"I wouldn't say that, but your father was intense and disciplined."

"Well, thanks, but I've learned from all of you, and I promise that I'll give your daughter all the love and tenderness that I've witnessed growing up."

"Hence the reason why I believed I'd be a grandfather in months instead of years," he chuckles. I'm glad I wasn't drinking because I would have spit it across their living room. He's referring to the fact that they all can't keep their hands off their wives, and he's right.

CHAPTER TWELVE

MELANIE

"OH MY GOD, DON'T STOP," I CRY OUT. HE FISTS MY HAIR, gripping it with such strength that it's almost too painful, and yet I can't get enough. Every thrust of his hips pushes his thick, enormous length deep into me, and I gasp as it hits my insides, brutalizing them like I've been a bad girl and I need to be punished. We fuck like wild animals, getting more and more aggressive as we gain experience and learn each other's bodies.

"I'm not going to stop. You're going to come and love it."

"Yes, please fuck me." I get it hard and fast, taking the pounding, and then my orgasm rips right through me, exploding like a tidal wave. It's so intense and long that it continues all the way through his release. My pussy spasms as he shoots his load inside me. I'm still shaking as he leans over me with his mouth on my shoulder.

"I love you so damn much."

I chuckle with my body still twitching. "I love you too, rough rider."

"Baby, next time you're the one going for a ride," he growls against my ear, biting it. "I'm going to have you riding my cock, soaking it while your tits bounce in my face."

"Maybe later tonight."

"You're right. I'm already late for work." He swats my ass and pulls out. "Damn, that is sexy."

"What is?"

"The sight of my cum just dripping down your pussy and making a pretty little mess." He grabs his cock, trying to stave off a growing erection.

"Get ready, horny slacker. Not all of us can just take time off. I have homework to do and an appointment at the salon."

"You don't need to get anything done. You're gorgeous as you are."

"Don't worry, I'm not dyeing my hair."

"As much as I love your color, Raven, if you did dye it, I wouldn't be upset. I support you in almost anything except another person in our relationship."

"That we can totally agree on. Mr. Steele, you are mine and only mine," I hiss, standing up and reaching up on my tiptoes to kiss his chin. "I'm going to miss you."

"We have time to shower together."

"No, we don't."

"We do if I say we do."

"Your father is going to really hate me."

"My father loves you. Now move your ass before I say that you debated getting in the shower with me and that was the holdup."

"You wouldn't."

"I most certainly would, and he'd be on my side." He winks and then quickly flips me onto his shoulder, hustling us into our master bathroom. With a giggle and then a spank to my bottom, I allow my soon-to-be husband to wash and lather me before going to work.

I STOP INTO THE SALON, WANTING TO GET MY HAIR PREPPED for the wedding with a nice treatment and to cut the ends, and unfortunately that bitch is there. I stroll in with my future mother-in-law, holding my head up high. There's no way I'll be intimidated by this woman who tried to steal my man and failed miserably. Taking a seat in the chair, Maria smiles. "How does the bride-to-be feel?"

"Wonderful, but we still have a month to go. I just need a quick healing mask. Between the heat and the pool, my hair is getting a little damaged."

"She's still gorgeous." I love my mother-in-law.

"Are you getting anything done today?"

"No, I'm just here to spoil my favorite daughter-in-law."

"I'm your only one." A scoff comes from the side, and we all turn our heads. Chrissy clears her throat and continues to sweep the floor.

"Since you're not doing anything, can you mix a protein mask for me?" My face freezes in terror at the thought of her mixing anything for me. Mrs. Steele just taps my shoulder.

"Whatever. I'll be back in a minute." She leaves us, and then I see them point to the cameras above. They can see if she does anything, but they won't be able to tell until it's too freaking late.

"What if...?"

"Don't worry." Maria pats my hand before brushing my hair.

Mrs. Steele continues to talk about my wedding and the plans we have to make. Two minutes later, Chrissy comes from the back room with the mixture in a bowl and a brush. She hands it over to Maria, and the front door slams open. The deputy comes in with Boomer and my father.

"Ms. Heath, you're fired, and you've just lost your license."

"What?"

"We have you on camera putting lightener in the bowl."

"What? You framed me."

"No, you were supposed to do your job, and you tried violate a client. You have a choice—to be arrested, or just leave."

"Fine, but I'm taking my things." She huffs toward her station while the deputy stays with her, keeping a close eye on her in case she does something crazy. Luckily the bitch only gives us some scathing looks before taking her leave. I don't know what happened after she left, but honestly, I've lost all enthusiasm about getting my hair done.

"What's wrong, sweetie?" my father asks.

"I just want to go home." I stand up and grab my purse.

"I'll take you." I see the remorse and pity in their eyes, but frankly, I just need to chill and not stress. It's not their fault because it's good to get rid of that crazy witch before she starts something when no one is around.

When I get home, Will pulls up and is out of his truck. "What are you doing here?" I ask.

"My father called."

"And you came home from work?"

"Raven, I'll always be there when you need me. I've got it from here," he tells my father, taking my hand and walking me into our house.

I wave goodbye to my father and he drives off, looking a little annoyed. "He thinks you've taken his place."

"In a way, I have. I'm now your main protector. They

should have told you about what they had planned instead of ambushing you like that."

"You knew?"

"No, of course I didn't. I wanted to have the bitch fired for just offering herself to me, but it wasn't my call."

"Will, will you take me riding?"

"You want to go riding?" His eyes light up. I nod, and he jumps up from our sofa, taking my hand. "Come on, beautiful, let's not waste this wonderful day together. I haven't had you on the back of my bike since you were sixteen."

"Yes, and we were at the lake with the guys."

"I was so pissed and horny, as I'm sure most of the guys were."

"They weren't." He scoffs and tilts his head in disbelief. "Is that why you gave me a ride home?"

"Yes. You were in a tiny bikini, flaunting that flat stomach, perky, luscious breasts, and round ass that belonged to me while smiling and giggling at them. I thought I was going to have a heart attack and have to kill half my cousins and friends. The damn traitors."

"Who told you I was there?"

"Connor."

"He's the one who invited me."

"He's a bastard. I'm really going to punch that bastard or hug him. He knew what the fuck he was doing when he did it. He wanted me to get you alone and on my bike. I'd been dreaming about it, craving it, and I told the fucker. My dick is so damn hard right now." I pause and rub my chin, thinking about skipping the ride and taking her sexy ass upstairs. Then again, another idea pops in my head.

"Do you still have that bikini?"

"Yes," I answered, smiling at him.

"Well, what are you waiting for, sexy?" He spins me around toward our staircase and swats my ass.

"So bossy. That might leave a mark."

"Good, then everyone who gets a glance at that fabulous ass before they die will know you're mine," he grunts before I run up the stairs, giggling all the way. I love the man with my entire being, and I can't wait until the day we're married. The day can't come fast enough. Sometimes I wonder why I decided to let our mothers go along and plan out this elaborate affair. Then again, I remember that I already live with him and the only thing missing is the title of Mrs. William Steele.

"Soon," I whisper and shake my head while getting dressed. The countdown to the wedding feels endless.

CHAPTER THIRTEEN

WILL

WAKING UP NEXT TO THE MOST BEAUTIFUL WOMAN IN THE world is perfection. Even my dreams are filled with Melanie and our future. "Why are you smiling?" she says, turning onto her stomach and resting her head on her elbows.

I turn to my side. "I was just thinking about how perfect our life is."

"It is fantastic," she sighs, running her dainty, talented hand across my chest. "What are your plans for today?"

"Well, after I spend the morning worshiping between your thighs, I plan to go to work and then take you to dinner. Then, we will spend the rest of the evening at home doing whatever you please."

"I'm starting to believe you take pleasure in making me happy, Mr. Steele."

"I'm glad you're finally seeing things my way, Miss Brandon." My lips brush down on hers, and as always, just the simple act sends me into a frenzy. I pull her onto me, straddling my body with her legs on either side.

"Wow, Mr. Steele, someone is happy to see me this morning," she teases, grinding her wet slit over my engorged length. Fuck—if my dick was out of my boxers, I'd already be filling her up.

"You know I'm always happy to see you, Raven."

"Show me." Suddenly my phone rings, killing the mood. It sucks that I have to answer it, but as the future head of the company and the Steele Riders, it's always important I do. She attempts to roll off me, but that shit won't fly. I slide my boxers down and slip the tip into her wetness, letting her work herself onto my meat.

As I answer, "Will here," I mouth a simple, "Ride me," and then pop her round ass.

"We have a situation at the clubhouse. I need you here as soon as possible," my father says.

"Yes, I'll be there in forty minutes." I hold back a grunt when Melanie rolls her hips, squeezing my dick.

"Where are you? Not on the site—it's Saturday."

"You just woke me up."

"You are the future president. You need to be here faster than that, Son. I need you here in twenty, pussy or not. Sorry, Beast." Shit, her father's there. Oops. I don't give a fuck, but I look at my woman who is taking my dick to the hilt. Melanie blushes and then starts working her pussy faster on my cock, bouncing up and down, biting on her bottom lip.

"Okay. Fuck," I groan, ending the call and tossing my phone across the room. "We can finish this later."

"Or we can finish this now," she moans. She's right. I sit up and cradle the back of her skull; her long dark hair slides through my fingers.

"Okay, Princess. Let's fuck," I grunt, sitting up further and sending my dick deeper.

"Fuck," she cries out. "You're so damn deep."

"That's right. Take that dick, baby, and come quick or I'm going to because I have to go to work." I fist her hair and make her bounce on me. Our mouths crash on each other, and our chests meet. Her pebbled nipples scrape against my skin, and I'm barely hanging on. "Fuck, be a good girl and come for me before I break."

"I am," she cries out, gripping my hair and tugging on it. "Rett," her voice echoes through our bedroom. "Shit, shit, oh. Rett." She clings to my hair as her back arches and her tight pussy clenches around my thick cock. Her orgasm spurs my own; like a vampire needing to feed, I bite down on her neck, growling and emptying my load into her pussy. I know we're protected, but every time I fill her up, I get the satisfaction that one day in the future she won't be and I'm the only one with that privilege.

"IT'S ABOUT TIME YOU SHOWED UP," MY DAD SAYS.

"Pops, it's only been twenty-one minutes. What's going on?"

"Someone broke into the clubhouse last night."

"What the fuck? And you're just finding this out now?"

"Our surveillance system was tampered with."

"So it was an inside job."

"We had a severe storm yesterday, so someone saw it as a perfect opportunity to use the downed power grid, the backup generator, and the lack of guards that were moved to protect the houses first. Whoever it was knew the contingency plans."

"Well, I have an idea who."

"Who?" my father asked.

"Who the fuck else? Damon. We kicked that fuck out instead of killing him like I wanted to. He was willing to double cross me for my woman, knowing damn well the consequences. Don't you think it would be possible that he'd be the one to access the clubhouse?"

"Where is he?"

"I don't know," Ian says. He's the tech that works with Cyber, who has been down with a serious stomach flu.

"Isn't it a coincidence that Cyber's severely ill, and then this happens? I'm calling Miles."

118

"We call Miles and we're going to have bloodshed before we know what's going down," Beast warns. "Won't just be the Riders. He'll have goons in here that rival the cartels." That's why I like Miles. He's a bit crazy and that's needed.

"If someone poisoned his father and we don't tell him, what do you think he'll do?"

"You're right," my dad says.

"Poisoned who?" Miles says, walking in the clubhouse. "You all need better security at the gate." He adjusts his bloody cuff.

"Tell me he's not dead."

"He's not dead," he answers with a deadpan expression.

"Seriously, Miles."

"Come, now, Uncle Boomer. I swear I didn't kill your pathetic foot soldier, but I did give him a warning that if he ever denies me entry again, I'll kill his entire family. I just found out my father is in the hospital. My private doctor is seeing him. Now—since you fucks want to leave me out of the shit storm that's apparently going down, I'm assuming you believe it's not just some foodborne illness."

"We believe he might have been poisoned so someone could hack our surveillance."

"I will locate the fuckers, and then I will hunt them down." On top of being an elite hacker, Miles is a mob boss. Natural-born psycho, it would seem. "Have you had this place swept for devices before you held a fucking meeting in here?"

"No."

"You're getting old." Miles tips his head toward the door. Moments later, several men exit a cluster of black SUVs.

"They're going to sweep the place for all devices. Someone wanted in here for more than security."

"I can hack into the system from my home in Vegas," he confesses. "What else is here? Codes to bank records? Buildings?" My father thinks about it all. There are lots of things in his office that are accessible, but he locks it up tight and without proper access, you can't get in once it's locked.

All of the men run out. "Sir, we need to leave now. It's rigged to explode."

"What?" We all shouted.

"The bomb is in the kitchen. It's rigged to the oven timer, and we only have a minute left." We don't even get to the main gate when there's a large explosion inside. The building rattles, and a plume of smoke comes from under the doors.

"It looks like it wasn't completely totaled, but we'll need to wait for a team to inspect it."

"Miles, they call me 'Boomer' for a reason. I'm a demolition expert, and so is my son. Someone did this intentionally, and they will pay for it."

Three hours later, we have the burning embers put out and finally deem the building safe to enter. Miles decided to leave almost immediately after we had things under control. He didn't want to leave his parents alone for even a moment. Most of the damage is to the kitchen and main hangout area, although they did manage to send a message to my father's office, creating a giant hole in the side of one wall. Thankfully, nothing but a sofa is there.

All the load-bearing walls are still standing, however my father wants to double down on the stability of the clubhouse, so there is an entire crew out here to work on it. He pulled them off another job, delaying the other project a week. Unfortunately, it will upset the client, but we don't give two fucks.

My father comes out of the central security area with his lead foreman and asks me, "Where is Miles?"

"At the hospital with his father."

"Do you think he's going to find whoever hacked our system and poisoned his father?" Beast asks.

"Have you met the crazy bastard?" I ask. My phone rings, and it's Melanie. Fuck. We've been so busy dealing with this that I didn't have time to call and inform her about what's going on.

"Shit, it's Melanie. What am I going to tell her?"

"Tell her there was a gas leak at the clubhouse. That's the story we're going to roll with. Our women don't need to know the problems. As much as you want to be honest with all this stuff, some of these problems don't need to rest on their tiny shoulders."

I nod, walking away from him, and call her back. "Sorry, baby. It's been pretty crazy here. There was a gas leak at the clubhouse, and it caused a decent-sized explosion in the kitchen area. My father and I are working with our team to deal with the clean-up and repair."

"Oh God. Please tell me no one was hurt."

"No, baby. Of course not. No one was here at the time, but I will see you later, okay? I'm sorry, but this may take all day and I'm going to be working hard to get this repaired so my men can get back to their other worksites."

"I understand. I have school on Monday anyway, so it's not like I'm not busy anyway."

"That's why I love you, beautiful."

"Because I have school?" she asks with an air of sass in the sexy voice of hers. I swear if I could get home and spank her, I would. My dick hardens in a second, and I don't have anywhere to hide it, so I walk over to the back of my work truck and adjust myself.

"No, smartass. Because you're reasonable and wonderful," I grunt into the phone.

"I'm only reasonable because you gave me a fabulous orgasm this morning." She's a damn seductress, but I love it.

"Then I'll make sure to keep you coming."

"That you better do," she giggles before hanging up the phone.

I get back to work and hope that Miles finds an answer for me soon so I can go back to my bride-to-be with a clear conscience and stiff dick.

CHAPTER FOURTEEN

MELANIE

IT'S BEEN A WONDERFUL FOUR MONTHS TOGETHER, AND school has kicked off to an interesting start, but I'm feeling a bit tired this morning. Maybe it's a shift in the weather. It's a little cooler today with the fall air, so I wrap my light sweater around my chest as the sun peeks through the trees.

Will slides his arm around my waist and brushes his lips against my temple. "You look so damn fine this morning. I'm going to miss you."

"Me too," I sigh. Our relationship hasn't grown stagnant in the least, so the time apart always feels like an eternity. A workday and school day for us drags on.

"As much as I'd love to stay with you longer, I have to leave," he grumbles against my ear. Things have been weird lately. Since the explosion at the clubhouse last week, we haven't gone out once. He's been so busy or tired. I know he's working overtime to make up for the repairs and getting his men back on their other projects, but something feels off.

For a brief moment, Beth's old taunts swim in my head that he's having an affair, but I quickly brush them off. It's silly. I've spoken to my mother and father about the explosion and the constant work at the clubhouse, so we all know Will's pulling long hours. I'm not just some naïve girl wanting to believe whatever her man says.

"I know. Have a good day," I insist, smiling at him. As much as I hate that he has to leave, I understand.

His mouth lands on mine for a deep, penetrating kiss. The moan that comes from me is so intense that he spanks my ass. "That is not fair, woman. It's going to be hard to drive like this." Will adjusts his cock and shakes his head before shuffling down the steps in a hurry to his truck. "Have a great day at school, and I'll meet you for dinner," Will says before hopping in his work truck. I'm so glad he's taking an earlier day for me.

God, he looks sexy as hell in his fitted, plain white tee and blue jeans. My body burns with need for him. I have another hour before I need to hit the road, so we're taking two different vehicles into Dallas today. Besides, he's going to be there all day, whereas I'll only be in the city until two.

I wave him off and then turn around and go inside with my cup of coffee. Goodness, we already feel like a married couple, and we're not even close yet. My mother and I have lots of planning to do over the next two weeks before the big day, and with every second that passes, I get more and more giddy.

My phone rings, and I swipe it from my back pocket. "Hey, Mom."

"We have another fitting tomorrow. Are you available to meet Crystal and me for lunch afterward?"

"Yes. I'd love it. I don't have any classes tomorrow, so that should be perfect."

"Yay! I'm so excited, sweetie." My mother's gushing only adds to my excitement. I jump about the kitchen, nearly sending my coffee splashing all over the counter.

I set it down and then add, "I can't wait either, Mom."

"Good. I can't wait. We'll drive together, then."

"Works for me. I've got to get to class, but I'll talk to you later." I hurry to class and get through two hours of lectures. It's time for one more class, but I decide to make a detour and head to the coffee shop. On the way, I give my bestie a call. "Hey, girl, how's it going? It's been a while."

"That's because you've been too busy with that player to talk to me anymore."

"Will's not a player. Why would you say that?"

"Come on. You moped about him for almost a full year, and you believe his lies so easily. I just don't see why you fell for it."

"Don't be like that. Will has been amazing and completely faithful."

"Just because he said so? That's so damn naïve," she says. Now I know why we stopped talking. She started ghosting me after being rude about my relationship with Will. She's really under the impression that Will cheated on me.

"Well, I'm off to the coffee shop on campus. Call me whenever. I miss you."

"Yeah."

I end the call, feeling a bit saddened, and want Will to tell me everything is going to be fine. *One more class, and then I can head home and get ready for dinner,* I mentally tell myself.

I'm halfway to get my coffee when I feel someone behind me, which isn't unusual given the campus is busy, but then a hand comes over my mouth and then I feel a prick in my neck. Slowly, I turn my head and recognize the eyes staring back at me. Shit. I brush my fingers over my father's bracelet, knowing it's his personal tracker on me, hoping it's still doing its job.

I cry out and try to fight, but my attacker isn't alone and before I can get my words out, the world darkens.

CHAPTER FIFTEEN

WILL

MELANIE WAS SUPPOSED TO BE HOME AROUND TWO-THIRTY OR three, given the traffic. I called her around that time because she never called me. My tracker shows her in Dallas, but nowhere near her car's tracker. My heart pounds out of control.

I call her security detail, Dusty. "Where's Melanie?"

He sighs and then says, "I lost her."

"What do you mean, you lost tabs on my Raven?" I bark into my phone. After everything that happened, I've been trying to remain calm. The hacker wasn't Damon because he wasn't sophisticated enough, but that didn't mean he didn't have help.

Miles had gotten a lead on the hacker, but then his issue was finding out who poisoned his father. The hacker intentionally bombed the clubhouse to delay the hacking notice.

"We can't find her," Dusty says.

"Don't fucking say that again. Give me an answer I want to hear, or you'll find out I'm crazier than my father."

"I was doing as you said, but I ran into her best friend, and we were talking when she spoke to Melanie, so I lost track of her for a bit. I assumed she had gone home when her car wasn't in the spot it had been in. I drove home, and it was gone."

"What friend?"

"The Beth friend. I ran into her at the campus, and she was just ending the call with Melanie." Beth goes to school there as well, but I didn't know they were still talking to each other. Melanie told me that Beth had been blowing her off lately.

I have my future father-in-law on the line before I waste another moment.

"What's going on?" he asks, breathing heavily.

"She's missing."

"What the fuck do you mean, she's missing?"

"Melanie's been taken. She's not answering her phone, and the tracker on her necklace isn't anywhere near her car."

"Fuck. She could be shopping," Beast says, trying to calm

me down. I'm flying down the road as fast as possible to get what I need for war.

He's not going to like the next part. "It's thirty miles away, but still in Dallas. I need an arsenal and a plan. I'm going to find my woman and whoever took her."

I hear him scrambling in the background. "I'm running her bracelet now." I knew the one she wore. It says *Daddy's Princess* on it.

"It's on campus."

"Where?"

"In the parking lot for the library sciences."

"Fuck, where her car is."

"So they took her."

"I need Cyber on the cameras for the college now, and I need all the Riders. I'm getting my future wife." They cleared him from the hospital and he's recovering, but I don't know if he can help us.

"They could have removed the necklace."

"No, they couldn't. Trust me—they can't. It's probably the only reason she's still wearing it." I drive over to my father's private cache of weapons and fill up my work truck, tucking them in the secret spots just as my father and brothers pull up beside me. "Someone's taken her."

"Who?"

"I have no idea, but I will find out. I can't fucking believe it." I slam my fist into the side of my truck, wanting it to be someone's face.

His phone rings. "It's Cyber." He answers, "Go ahead."

"Her phone is dead," Cyber says, his voice hoarse from the illness. "It's not responding. Signal lost on campus." He's typing in the background. "I've hacked that lot's visual, and you're going to be pissed. You should have killed him when you had a chance."

"Damon," I snarl. One dumb mistake, and this asshole could take away the love of my life. My entire body vibrates with rage. I don't care what happens to me as long as I get my hands on that son of bitch. Seeing the life leave his eyes is the only thing I can think about. Closing my eyes, I send up a silent prayer that my love is holding strong and that she's waiting for me to come get her.

"Yeah, and he had help," Cyber adds. "I couldn't make out the other people, but he had at least four others, and one was female by the build."

"How did they get away with it on campus?" my dad asks.

"It was an empty spot, and rain had started coming down just in time to create an isolating space. She was completely alone." Completely alone? I should kick my own ass. Guards should have been breathing down her back. I knew the danger over the past week, but I didn't want to scare her, so I tried to play it off. This is what I get. Fuck.

"They're all dead," I say, teeth grinding.

"It looks like they drugged her. I couldn't see what they did, but they tossed something before throwing her into an SUV. I have the tags and am running the plates. Miles is on his way to meet you. You'll need him and his men."

"Thanks. I'll appreciate their assistance."

"I'm out," I snarl, rushing to my truck.

"We're coming with you."

"We can't all go."

"Beast," my father says, and I turn just as I see him speed up behind me, slamming on his brakes and jumping out of his vehicle with his son.

"Tell me you have some fucking clue."

"It was that piece of shit you all didn't let me kill." I want to punch him in the face, but he loves her as much as I do.

"Well, he's a dead man now, and whoever has their hands in this will bleed out. Mary's a wreck." Shit.

"How does she know?" my father asks.

"We were busy when you called." He clamps his mouth shut, and at once I understand what the heavy breathing was about. They were fucking.

"Oh."

"Miles and his men will meet us at the location. We're going to ambush these fucks, but remember, we need to get Melanie out safe."

"Of course. Nothing happens to my baby girl. Will, I wish I'd let you kill that fucker. My gut knew it then, but I've grown soft."

"Let's hope we make it through this, and we can deal with it later. I need to find my fiancée."

We break out into different vehicles and drive off together, making our way toward the site. Miles has a plan, and I agree because he's crazy, and sending his men in first leaves our people safe. Besides, he wants to avenge his father. As long as he saves that piece of shit for me, everything else doesn't matter.

CHAPTER SIXTEEN

MELANIE

MY EYES FEEL SO HEAVY, AND MY HEAD IS FUZZY. I CAN'T seem to think straight. *Where am I?*

"Somewhere no one can find you." Shit, I said that out loud. My head's swimming, and I can't see anything but blurred shadows.

The voice vibrates in my head as the footsteps grow louder. "I'm going to have so much fun with you," I hear.

"Oh, no," I cry out, my voice hoarse and dry.

"Fuck, how much did you give her? I'm not fucking a corpse. I want to stare into her eyes and watch her pain as I take her little ass." Fear and fatigue mixed with whatever they gave me causes me to pass out again.

The smell of seafood is making me sick. Where the hell am I? What did they drug me with? If I make it out of here,

I'm never having fish again. Damn it, the pieces of shit ripped my father's bracelet from my wrist and stole my engagement ring. I'm still wearing my necklace, though, because they couldn't get it off my neck. The pieces of shit are pissed, and it shows on my throat. Tears well up in my eyes.

It's pointless to think my dad and Will can find me now. The ring has been taken and will probably be sold for a fortune, which it's probably worth. God—Will is going to be raging, and my parents will be devastated when they find my lifeless body, although I'm not sure what Damon's plan was in the first place. Hell, I wonder if he even knows.

"Well, well, well. Look who finally woke up." My eyes focus and my hearing is clear as hell, but I still can't believe this bitch is involved.

"Holy fuck, the doorknob's in on this?" I question.

"What the fuck did you call me?" Her voice hits a high, screeching echo like we're in some warehouse.

"Oops, did I say that out loud? Sorry, the brain's a little scrambled with all the drugs you fuck-offs filled me with." If her voice wasn't brutal enough, now my head is pounding out of control.

"You have such a smart mouth. I wonder how much your stupid pussy fiancé will pay to have it back in one piece." Goodness, I hate this double-wide-hole cunt with everything in me.

"Chrissy, do you think he'll pay you to have me back?"

"I'm counting on it. Although, after he sees what I did to you Damon's not sure, but he doesn't understand how pathetic Will is." She laughs maniacally.

I grasp my head and feel around, and that explains why my head hurts. My hair has been cut off. It's short like a bob in some places and shorter in others, but when I see the longest strands I cry, but not from sadness. My rage builds inside me like a silent storm brewing in the night, ready to unleash violent havoc in its wake. My hair is an orangish-yellow color with hints of black and brown, spotted like a calico cat. This bitch bleached my hair.

I'm in tears as she rambles on, chest heaving as I work up the strength to use my limbs again. I was so drugged up that they hadn't bothered to tie me down. It was a foolish mistake on her part. "Damon thought you were just property to the boss's son, but he doesn't understand that a man who turns away free pussy to save himself for mediocre virgin cunt is so whipped he'd do anything for it."

"Then you know he'd kill for it too," Will's voice rips through the warehouse, and both relief and dread fill me. What is he going to think when he sees me? Will he still want me? None of that matters at the moment, because I have to fight and get this crazy whore.

Within seconds, everything changes. Three men come out from the other side of the room. The knob slobberer screams, and the sound of gunfire tears through the building. I drop down and look for that bitch because no matter what happens, I want her head in the concrete until she stops breathing, and that's something I never thought I'd say or feel.

On the ground is a broken plastic chair with metal legs that must be from the fighting, so I snatch up one of the legs and stay hunched down, looking for my target. My eyes recognize Will's stance, so I peer upward for a moment, and the expression on his face is shock. I duck my head as the pang of sadness and anger fills me.

Now more determined than ever for revenge, I hunt through the haze and chaos around me until I spot her feet and direct my gaze upward. The cunt is trying to hide, but she messed with the wrong woman.

I take the rod and aim for my target. "You crazy bitch, this is for everything you did."

I lunge at her and she sticks her hands out, crying and let's out a screaming plea, "No, don't. I'm pregnant." I stop mid-flight, my own humanity taking over. As I back away, she smirks and then runs at me, but this time I don't feel sorry and I swing at her, sending her backward onto the cold floor.

"Fuck yeah," Miles cheers. "I was about to shoot that bitch." A shot rings out near us. "I'll be back," he says, smirking before running off.

I'm just about to move when I hear Damon and Will and my panic sets in.

CHAPTER SEVENTEEN

WILL

WE BARGE INTO THE WAREHOUSE IN THE FISHERY DISTRICT, ready for war. The bastards thought they could hold my woman captive and threaten her without retribution, but they were mistaken. As the words spill from Chrissy's lips, the rage doubles in me. Then I look in horror as I see what they did to my woman. The closer I get, the more shocked I become. They dared to hurt her so brutally, and it was my fault. The marking on her neck had been caused by the necklace I gave her.

I watch the way she ducks her head and see her turmoil. My woman has found her own personal demons, and after I slay these tangible ones, I have to find a way to destroy those invisible ones. One by one, Damon's men fall, little pussies who I recognize as a local gang in Dallas. They were probably hired to do his dirty work, which fucking sucks because we are creating a host of new enemies with this war. Still, I'd burn this city to the ground for my woman.

One by one, bodies fall to the ground, but I want one head above all, and that is Damon's, the piece of shit who took my woman in the first place. The man who thought he had a right to touch the most precious thing in the world and then harm her. Melanie belongs to me, and anything that happens to her is worth killing for. I've never had to get my hands this dirty, but there's nothing I won't do for my heart and soul.

"Looks like I have something you want," he says with a smirk.

I stare down the motherfucker and although he appears tough, standing closer to Melanie than I am, he doesn't have the resolve that I do. It's written all over his face. Fear washes over him, and it fills the air like a terrible aroma. I want to rip his heart out with my hands for the way my love has been treated, but his death will be enough for me. I hate him with everything in me, but her safety and care are all I need.

"Damon, this is between you and me."

"Oh, this is much bigger than you and me, playboy. You fuck around and break young girls' hearts, and now you have the audacity to be upset about the one whore that I took." At first I'm confused, but the insult to my wife sends me over the edge. I don't bother wasting time with his nonsense. I want revenge and to make him pay, but now that we're here, Melanie needs me more.

This isn't some movie where the fucking villain gets a damn monologue. I put a bullet in his head, and his body dropped. I already know he's working with the stupid bitch from the salon, and I haven't broken any hearts.

After he falls, I kick his gun away and rush to Melanie's side, picking her up in my arms. She's been through so much that I hate myself more than I can say. Will she still love me for not protecting her? Fuck. I see the wounds and know they wouldn't be there if I'd strangled Damon the first time I wanted to do it.

"Son, it's time to go." Something feels off about all of this, and I can't figure it out. How did they know about her classes and schedule? Who else was helping Damon and Chrissy? It's not like she had a tail on the way to school. Someone in town would have noticed it. Her security detail was light, but it's not nonexistent.

Who knows Melanie's routine as well as her team? Just me, and maybe her parents. Unless they were stalking her, and only one other person comes to mind, but I hope not for Melanie's sake. *The call and the security break-in.*

CHAPTER EIGHTEEN

MELANIE

His arms remain wrapped around me as Will's father drives us back to Steeleville where Doc is waiting at the hospital to tend to my wounds. I refused treatment at a Dallas hospital, and I could see both relief and concern on their faces because of it. They didn't want the added questions, but the wait to assess my damage would take longer.

Will hasn't uttered a word the entire ride, and his father looks through the mirror several times with questioning eyes. Slowly, I pull away from my fiancé—or should I say former fiancé, since there isn't a ring any longer—and the lack of words emanating from his lips says more than he knows.

My heart cracks. "Will, you can't blame yourself," his father says.

"The fuck I can't," he snarls. "I should have killed that bastard when I had the chance, and I needed to keep guards I trusted on her at all times." He turns to me, looking me over with such sadness in his eyes. Taking my hand in his, he asks, "Can you ever forgive me for what they did to you? I know that your hair will grow back, but the abuse and pain you suffered was unbearable. Your neck wound is all my fault. They could have strangled you to death because they couldn't get that damn thing off."

I take my hand from his and ask, "Is that why you were so disgusted back there?"

"Melanie, please tell me you're not serious?"

"I thought you were horrified by me."

"My sweet raven. You'll always be my raven, even if you had chosen to dye your hair blonde. I don't love you, crave you, need you just because of your gorgeous hair. I've always loved you and always will."

Even though he says it, I'm still skittish to fall into his arms. My fears are strong, but Will is stronger, and I find myself picked up and wrapped in his embrace. "Don't push me away. Whatever happens, we're in this together. Please. I beg of you, Melanie."

"I'll try," I answered with a sob, pressing my face into his shoulder.

His lips graze my cheek. "Rest. We'll be there soon."

The next thing I know, I'm at the Steeleville Hospital being brought in through a private entrance, and Dr. Grace, Uncle Ghost's wife, is seeing me. "Hey, Jelly Melly. I hear you were causing a ruckus today. I'm going to send these guys out."

"Do you want us to leave?"

"I think it would be best," Dr. Grace says.

"Can you call my mom?" I ask.

"Of course," Will says, nodding his head and stepping out of the room. The door closes, and she's handing me a gown.

"I'm going to need your clothes, and I have to ask the questions."

"I don't know what they did to me if you're asking, but I don't believe they raped me. I recall him saying he wanted me awake when he violated me, but they'd drugged me too much."

"I suppose we can count our blessings."

She's right about that. "I suppose so."

I get undressed as she preps her equipment and makes some notes. "Let me examine your head first."

"Can you check the other parts first? I need to be sure."

She smiles and squeezes my hand. "Absolutely." It's uncomfortable, but once she's done, she smiles and says, "There's no evidence of assault, Melanie. I did a swab just to be sure, but since you were unconscious, he would have had to had used a great deal of lubrication to get inside you or there would have been serious damage. There's no new bruising either." I blush at the word "new." With all the kinky fucking we've been doing lately, it's a wonder I'm not waddling most days. I've been feeling saddle sore, but I didn't want anyone else to know, so I've been trying to keep my gait normal.

"Thank you." I feel like a weight is lifted off my shoulders. Quickly, I cover myself when she stands.

"You're welcome. Let me check your neck and wrists, and then we'll get to your head. You can wrap the sheet over you if you feel more comfortable. I know this feels extremely invasive after everything that's happened today."

After everything is done, I ask for Will.

He enters the room looking like he's aged several years. "Babe," he whispers, sighing as he runs his hand through his smooth brown hair. "How are you feeling?"

"They gave me some painkillers, so right now I'm feeling pretty good," I answered, giving him a playful smile and wide eyes. He chuckles lightly.

"I...can...Melanie, can I hold you?"

"I'd love that," I say, nodding rapidly with my arms out, needing his touch more than I care to admit. He sits on the bed and lifts me onto his lap, holding me close. "I should have never went to get coffee," I sob against his chest.

"God, I love you so much. I was so damn scared that I'd lost you for good. Damn it, I don't know what I'd do without you. You're everything to me, my beautiful love." He kisses my temple and then clings to me. "Please tell me if I'm squeezing too tightly." As much as it hurts, I need his embrace to feel safe. Goodness, I don't feel protected without him. Have I developed a serious case of codependency? I don't care, because William Steele is my world.

"Thank you for finding me."

"Thank you for hanging on." His lips brush mine, and we fall into a sweet, gentle kiss before there is a knock at the door and the doctor comes in to check on me.

CHAPTER NINETEEN

WILL

WHEN BEAST'S EYES LAND ON HIS DAUGHTER'S BRACELET, I watch his jaw tighten. Then his eyes lift to meet mine. "You're a dead man, Will," my brother chuckles beside me.

I look over at my blushing woman and give her a wink. "She's no longer Daddy's Princess. She's Will's Property." I smirk at my soon-to-be father-in-law and take a pull of my beer. He's lucky I don't tattoo it on her because I'm tempted as fuck. The trouble that she put me through and the shit I did made it all the more real, and claiming her has been the most important thing on my brain. She belongs to me like I belong to her.

I want everyone to know it. There's no way it will go unnoticed now. Soon, everyone will see it in a different way. In a few years, her belly will be rounded as fuck. I have plans for her that her father won't approve of, but I don't care because I did what he didn't, what he couldn't. I protected her. She's mine.

"Tomorrow's your wedding. Are you ready?" my father asks. That's a dumb question and he knows it, but I think he enjoys teasing me. After all, it's the rehearsal dinner, and we have a bunch of guests around to try and mess with me.

"Of course. I live with the love of my life, and all I want to do is make sure she's mine in every way. Well, in almost every way. One day we'll start a family, but I'm in no hurry for that."

"One day, we'll all be ready for grandkids, but I'm glad you're waiting because your sisters are driving me nuts and I can't imagine them having boyfriends yet. Beast is enjoying the subtle digs about them finding husbands the second they turn eighteen."

"Yeah, well, it's better than them sleeping around at sixteen with some limp little bitch in high school who is just going to dump them and move on to the next girl. I get that Melanie is too young to get married, but it's not going to change a thing."

"It will take time for him to get used to it."

"Will, may I have a word with you?" Beast asks, stepping up to us. He's in a well-tailored suit. It's truly a wonder he is in the Riders in the first place, having been an attorney all these years.

"What's up?" I say.

"I saw the bracelet, but her necklace is gone. Please tell me it isn't because of the attack."

"It is, but the bracelet is made of the same material, and they can't strangle her should someone dare lay their hands on her again."

"You can't think like that. She loves that necklace; you know that, and I know it. Don't let the fears get to you. As a man obsessed with his wife, I'll tell you that there will always be times you'll worry, but it doesn't mean you take away the things that make them happy."

"I can't let her be hurt like that again. They nearly choked her to death because of it."

"No, they probably wanted to choke her. The charm could have been broken, but they didn't bother doing so. I'm happy that you love her, even if it's a bit unnerving how strong that love is. Still, her happiness matters most to me."

"Understood." I nod, and then he pulls me in for a hug.

"Congratulations, son," he whispers. I stare at my beloved Melanie over his shoulder, who smiles radiantly.

THE VEIL COVERS HER FACE AND HAIR, SENDING A GROWL through my chest and out my throat. I don't like her covered up in my presence. As she reaches the altar, I lift the offending thin fabric from her gorgeous face, and I'm so stunned by her natural beauty that my heart nearly stops. They've styled her short hair into a pixie cut, and it's dyed close to her natural black hair color. "Wow, you are perfect, Melanie."

"You're just saying that because it's our wedding day."

"I'm saying what I see. Now marry me, woman, before I lose my mind."

She blushes so perfectly that I can't wait to get this over with so I can show her what she does to me. "Well, Mr. Steele, I'm waiting." She turns to the priest and takes my hand.

"If anyone objects to the marriage, speak now or forever hold your peace."

"I object," a woman's voice comes from the back of the church.

"Beth?" Melanie gasps. She's dressed in a white dress that's so damn similar to Melanie's I could swear it's the same one. "What are you doing here?"

"I told you not to marry him." She's holding a bouquet of flowers, but I don't trust it. Dusty is right behind her. I nod to him. "You were supposed to choose Damon, and you didn't. I threw him in your face for months. I made excuses. If that stupid bitch Chrissy didn't get in the way, my plan would have worked, and you wouldn't have taken my man. You just have to have everything, don't you, Melanie? Well not anymore." She stretches out the arm of her bouquet, but Dusty tackles her to the ground. The gun flies out of her hands and across the church to the altar. Beast snags it and tucks it away.

"So now you know who else was involved," he tells me.

"You thought someone else was in on my kidnapping?" Lanie gasped, clutching my arm.

"It just didn't make sense that they knew where you were. You told me that you went to get coffee and, well, they couldn't have anticipated your detour."

She gasps, allowing reality to sink in. I hold onto the love of my life because there's no way in hell I'll let her crash now. She looks up at me and smiles. "Thank you, but I promise, Mr. Steele that I am perfectly fine."

Law's deputy arrives five minutes later to take Beth out of the church in handcuffs. As the commotion begins to settle, Beast says, "Well, no offense, but since these two have waited long enough, how about we get this show on the road?"

"I couldn't agree more. Ms. Melanie Brandon, will you marry me?"

"I would love nothing more."

The ceremony is quicker than I expected, and I'm now the proud husband of Melanie Steele. The world has finally been set right in my eyes as I stare at the most beautiful woman, and we belong to each other.

The celebration doesn't last long because we have to deal with the uproar that Beth created. She went on and on about Damon's plan to kidnap Melanie and how she helped them and that we probably killed him. Luckily, the only people to hear her outlandish comments were the cops who worked with us.

Damon's death had been ruled legal in the rescue attempt of the daughter of a government official off a public college campus. Of course the shooting didn't quite take place there. We moved it to the outskirts of Steeleville where our men could handle the bodies, while Miles men cleaned up the warehouse on the docks.

Chrissy didn't survive the transport, but that wasn't Melanie's fault. Let's just say not all of Miles' men are forgiving. I reassured Mel that the bitch only lied about being pregnant to so she'd let her guard down. Frankly, I'm glad she's dead because that's one last problem to worry about. If Beth is going to be an issue, she'll have to go as well.

"Stop frowning, son," my mother strolls in. "Your guests are going to think you made a mistake."

"I'm supposed to be enjoying my reception, but I've just got back from the police station with that crazy bitch trying to ruin everything."

"What? Didn't you hear what just happened? She can't ruin everything anymore."

"What?"

"Beth wasn't completely disarmed before she got in the back of the police car. She had pills stashed. She popped them after we left. She killed herself."

"Are you serious?"

"Yes," she says with a sigh.

"That's good and terrible. Where's Melanie?"

"She's with her father." My mother points toward the dessert table where Melanie pretends to straighten the already perfectly organized treats. Her emotions were visible on her gorgeous face. I could get lost just staring, but she needs more than that. She needs me and I need to act like the husband I signed up to be. The one she deserves.

"I need to tell her." I pass my mother and walk over to my wife who looks as if she's barely holding it together. Her father steps back, understanding it's now my place to step in. I give him a respectful nod and he walks away.

I whisper, "Raven."

Her tear-filled eyes meet mine. "It's all my fault."

Cradling her face, I stare into her beautiful eyes and tell her the truth that she needs to hear. "No, it's not. Don't say that shit."

She shakes her head, scrunching her eyes shut and refusing to believe me. "First Chrissy and now Beth."

"If that's the case, baby then it's all my fault. They were after me not you."

"I killed them," she hisses under her breath. I pressed her to my chest.

"No, you didn't. No, you didn't. Come take a walk with me, Mrs. Steele." I take my beautiful wife's hand and lead her outside the reception area. It's a gorgeous night; the breeze is just perfect with the fall leaves beginning to land on the ground. It would be a wonderful day if it wasn't for the mess that those we buried had created.

"My beloved Raven, Chrissy died because they refused to allow her a chance to attack you again. That was their choice, not yours. I agree with them. If you had let her attack you that day, Miles or myself would have killed her then.

"When it comes to Beth, your father had gotten more information from her parents. There's a reason they cut ties with her. Those bastards knew how crazy she was. I wasn't the first guy she'd gotten obsessed with. You weren't the first woman she'd gotten close to or the first she tried to kill. Her real name is Elizabeth Anne Smith and she's twenty-one not eighteen."

She gasps, knees buckling. "I can't believe it."

"Yeah, I know."

"That's not what I mean. One day I was over, I saw the ID and she nearly freaked on me, but then she quickly corrected herself and said it was her fake ID to get into clubs in Dallas."

"I'm sorry."

"Don't be sorry. It's my fault for introducing her into our lives."

"No, it's her parents. They tried to deny what their daughter was, and they got her out of trouble the first time. They thought she was safe, but she wasn't on her meds."

"Enough," Melanie huffs, throwing her hands down at her sides. "I want to celebrate us. I don't want to deal with anyone else's problems. We made it and we had an entire banquet hall full of hundreds of people there for us. Let's go in and cut our cake, dance, and then you can strip me bare and worship Mrs. William Steele."

"I can't agree more." I scooped her up and carry her back inside with loud cheers as we enter.

EPILOGUE

WILL

FIVE YEARS LATER

HER EYES CLOSE, TEETH CLENCHED OVER HER BOTTOM LIP AS I pump hard into her, slamming my hips until we're fully connected. Damn, Melanie's body is made for me, and no one can tell me otherwise. Five years together, and we still fit like a glove. My hands flex on her hips, gripping them firmly, holding her down as I drill her pussy. Every time I mark my territory, I want to do it again. My poor wife has no idea how obsessed I am with her. All these years, and I'm just as nuts as I was when I first realized I loved her—if not more.

"Come for me. Let me feel that tight pussy clench around my big cock. Squeeze me dry, and then come all over and soak me."

"Fuck. Breed me, Will," she shouts, gripping my biceps and digging her nails into me. "I want your babies. Fill me up, now."

I growl, pumping faster, spurred on by her words. I've been aching to get her pregnant, wanting everyone to see that she's mine in all ways. "I'm gonna come in your tight little hole until you're swollen with my boys, my raven. Be careful what you ask for."

"I've been off birth control for a month, Mr. Steele. Do your worst."

I punish her womb, fucking her pussy rough, going out of control like a fucking savage. Her moans drive me on. I've never been more aroused as I fuck my wife. We both lose our minds until I empty my seed inside her.

"Fuck, I'm coming, Melanie."

"That's it. Breed me." My big cock rams her, beating that hole until I've got nothing left. She cries out, screaming my name, nails digging into my back as she clings to my body.

"Thank you, baby."

"No, thank you. That was wonderful, Will." She sighs. "I can't believe how wild you got today."

"The thought of you having my baby just set me off." I chuckle and then attack her neck, kissing her before pinning her for another round.

"Will, I'll be pregnant in no time." She giggles.

"Good," I answer with a deep thrust.

EPILOGUE

WILL

TWO MONTHS LATER

"Beautiful, what's with that look?" She saunters into the kitchen as I take a drink of my coffee. I'm about to meet my dad and some of the Riders for a long ride for the day.

"I just want you to be careful this morning."

"I'm always careful. Do you want to ride with me?" She's planning to hang with our mothers and sisters this morning. It's just going to be a guys' trip today, but I'd rather have her on the back of my bike.

"I think I should be a little extra careful for the time being."

"What do you mean?"

"Um…" She digs into her jeans and pulls out a little stick, handing it to me. My mouth falls open because I don't need to guess what it is to know the damn answer, but I still look at it.

"I'm going to be a daddy." I throw my arms around my gorgeous wife of five years and spin her around.

"I take it you're pleased, Daddy?"

"More than pleased," I growl along the shell of her ear. My dick throbs against my jeans.

"You have to leave and meet with the guys," she reminds me, and for the first time, I don't want to go out for the usual long ride with the guys.

"Damn. How am I going to keep this to myself?"

"You don't have to save it," she says with a knowing grin.

"You don't want to tell them together?"

"We can go to your parents' together now, and then I'll stay with your mom, and you'll ride out."

I follow behind my wife as she drives to my parents', who are going to lose their minds. Hell, her parents are going to be there as well, and I can sense they're itching for the same thing. She doesn't exit the cab of the truck until I reach the driver's side. I lift her out of the vehicle and pull her in for a kiss, slipping my hands over her ass and squeezing her sweet bottom.

"I don't think I'll ever get used to this," Beast grumbles from the porch.

"Daddy," she squeals, jumping out of my arms.

"Hey, I thought that was my title," I said, earning a growl from my father-in-law.

"Aren't you too young for that type of kink?"

"It's not a kink." I slide my hand around her belly, rubbing it.

His eyes widen, and the realization hits him. "I'm about to be a grandfather?"

She nods and smiles.

"What's going on out there?" my Pops says.

"You didn't tell me shit," Beast says. "Your mother will kill us all."

"Hi, Pops. Beast is just giving me shit for kissing my wife."

"Yeah, I don't think I'll ever get over a man wanting my little girls," he huffs, walking into the house.

"You have a few more years at least." Beast bumps my dad's shoulder and chuckles.

"Let's hope a decade," he grumbles.

It's nice to see that their friendship wasn't harmed in all this. If anything, it's gotten closer. I'm sure they're going to be fighting over who is going to teach the kids how to ride first or who gets to babysit. They may be giant, rough men, but underneath, they are great family men who I've learned everything from. I only hope I'm half the man they are.

"So mom, Momma Steele, Will and I have something to tell you." Melanie bites down on her lip so damn adorably I'm sure they've already figured it out, but they haven't said a word. My mother-in-law is already sitting on the edge of her seat, nearly jumping off her chair. My mom's perfectly shaped brows are full of tension as she stares at us, waiting impatiently. Our dads are standing behind them because her Beast knows and doesn't want to give it away and I'm betting my father isn't a fool either.

"Well, what is it?" my mother asked, eyes wide with anticipation.

"We're having a baby," we say together.

"About time," my mom shouts, popping out of her seat.

"Yes," Mrs. Brandon cries, pulling my wife into her arms. "I love you, baby girl. Congratulations."

"Thank you."

"Son, I'm so happy for you," my father said, pulling me in for a quick embrace. I pull back and he's fighting tears. "Damn, I'm getting old."

"Yeah, but I can't say I blame ya, Boomer. All this time I've been waiting for them to tell us when they'd add to the family already. Congrats, Will." My father-in-law shakes my hand and then smiles before walking over to his baby girl.

His phone rings as he pulls away from me. I know it's the crew, wondering why we're taking so long to get to the clubhouse. "So are you ready for that ride or do you want to sit this one out?"

"As much as I want to stay and celebrate, Melanie doesn't want me to miss out on it."

"You men, go and have your ride. Pretty soon he'll end up missing some of them as I get too big, and he'll be too worried to travel."

"You're right about that," I grumbled, pulling her into my arms. They all chuckled, but not at me. Everyone had been in our shoes before at one time or another. With all the kids just popping out everywhere, there were times that they couldn't take long rides.

EPILOGUE

MELANIE

FIVE YEARS LATER

"Daddy," Andrea calls out. "Daddy, where are you?" I quickly adjust my dress while Will fixes his pants.

"This is your fault," he growls against my ear as I can feel his seed slide into my panties.

"Mine?" I challenged, giggling as I pressed my hand against his chest. "You're the one who pulled me in here." We were at the clubhouse trying to get stuff done before the annual picnic, but even after ten years of marriage we get carried away.

"You're the one who came in here with that damn dress. How is a man supposed to get any work done when his gorgeous wife comes in here looking like a fuckable piece of ass, needing to be marked up?" he growls, cupping my neck, giving me one more kiss before patting my bottom.

I open the office door to my little mini-me. "Aren't you supposed to be with Grandpa, little miss?" I asked her.

Andie walks past me and straight up to Will, "Grandpa told me that you are incooour-rrig-able."

"Do you mean incorrigible?" he questions our four-year-old fairy princess who is dressed in a pink tutu and black leather jack with pigtails and pink and black Converse and crazy cool black and pink fairy wings.

She tilts her head to the side with her hand on her hip, twisting her lips. "Yep, and that Grandpa William is on his way."

"Thank you, sweetheart. I'm going right now." She nods and then turns on her heel and sasses her way back out to Boomer. She has so much personality and is starting to learn things every day.

"Well, that is a close one, Lanie."

"You're telling me. Let's go wash up before my father gets here." We head to the bathroom and make it out in time as my father pulls up. He comes bearing gifts for Andrea.

"Andie Candy, my sour apple, were you a good girl today?" he asks her. She smiles so sweetly, but we know she is not. She told him that before and that's why he calls her sour apple.

"Yes, Grandpa, but Daddy and Mommy were in trouble."

"Oh yeah?" he says, cocking his brow with a smirk.

I was about to cover her mouth, but she got the words out first. "Daddy called Mommy a bad girl and he spanked her in Daddy's office. I told Grandpa. He said Daddy is ingorr-gg-gable." It's not the Texas sun that turns my face a nice shade of red. Out of the mouths of babes.

"Come on little terror, let's go harass, Pops." He takes the little blabber mouth out of the room, and I feel better, but now it's just me and my father. When I look back at him my face is flush with embarrassment.

He chuckles, laughing so the crinkles in his eyes show. He's older, but my father is still a very handsome man. "Come on now, Princess. You have two little ones and you've been married for ten years now. I think I figured out how you two got them."

"And how we made this one, too," I confessed, rubbing my belly.

"What? You're going to have another baby?"

"Yes." My smile is a mile wide, matching my father's.

"Congrats." My father hugs me and then pulls back. His face pales and I'm surprised because he should be happy for us. "Are you trying to get me murdered? Why am I always the first parent to find out? Your mother is going to be upset when she learns."

"Learn what?" We both whip our heads toward my mother who looks lovely as ever with her hands on her hips and her brow raised.

I walked up to her and took her hands in mine, giving

them a squeeze. "Mom, Will and I are having another baby."

"I thought so."

"You did?"

"Yes, I saw the both of you coming out of the doctor's office yesterday and you were grinning from ear to ear. Will pressed his hand to your stomach. I was waiting for you to say something." She yanks me in for a hug. "Goodness, you were a bad girl," she says after sniffing me. "Maybe take a shower."

"Gross."

"I'm talking about how she smells like men's cologne." She slaps my father's arm. "Where is my little man at?"

"He's napping in his play yard." I point over to the secured area where little Garrett sleeps. He's nearly two years old and resting after running around all morning. As if on cue, he begins moving.

"He must know his favorite Grandma is here."

"Yes, he does," Crystal says, coming in through the door with a laugh.

"Oh lord, babe. It looks like we're going to have to give them ten kids to make them happy," Will says, walking back in. His dad is carrying Andrea who is now holding an ice cream.

"Where did she get that?"

"From the outside cooler," Will says, pointing to my father-in-law. He's been working on the grill.

"Grandpa said I earned it," she says with a smirk, licking it with attitude.

"She conned it out of him," Jackson says entering the clubhouse with a tray of food, Penny following behind.

"He's getting soft in his old age," my dad says.

"Look who's talking. You gave her a cookie before dinner yesterday even after I told her no." I glared at my father. He wouldn't have dared let us get away with that when we were kids.

"Don't be upset, Melanie. We do it for the grandkids too," Penny says, giving me a hug. "One day, you'll do it, too. Now come and pick out your favorites before the hoard snatches them. I want my future grandniece or nephew well-fed and spoiled."

I shake my head and giggle, walking over to the dessert bar set up on the bar top inside the clubhouse away from the heat. How it spread already is amazing, but then I remember Will was outside with his father and mother who we told this morning. I wasn't going to burst my father's bubble, but I was sick and they saw, so they caught on. Either way, I'm happy that Will and I are adding to our growing family.

"What's on your mind, my lovely Raven?" Will asks, sliding his hand around my waist and nibbling on my neck. Goodness, we just finished a fast round in his office and I swear I'm just as riled up and ready for another wherever he'd like to take me. These ten years together haven't dulled my lust for my husband.

My mother had been right. I remember seeing my dad chasing my mother in the kitchen and wondering if she played hard to get because she really didn't want it or because she enjoyed the chase. We talked about it recently and it was the thrill of being pursued. I loved it. Will could hunt me down any time he'd like.

"Nothing but joy. Now, let me pick my goodies," I huff, pretending to be annoyed with his touch.

"I know what I want."

"Which ones?" I asked.

He growls and nibbles on my neck. "You're all the sweetness I need. Forever."

"Later, Mr. Steele. Later."

He bites my neck and then slaps my ass, whispering, "Always," as he walks away.

ALSO BY C.M. STEELE

A Best Friends Duet:

Picture Perfect * Instant Obsession

Best Friends Series:

Always You * His Dirty Secret * Sleep Tight

Bianchi Crime Family:

Married to the Mob * Captured by the Mob * Owned by the Mob

Cavanaugh Security Series:

Protecting Macy * Securing Blake

The Cline Brothers of Colorado:

Whatever it Takes * Taking Whatever He Wants
* Finding Paradise

The Conti Crime Family Series:

Alessio * Dario * Enrico * Matteo * Gio

Dirty Boss Series:

My Pet * My Cookie * My Flower * My Valentine

(Now on Audio)

The Falling Hard & Fast Series:

Falling for the Boss * Falling for the Enemy * Falling Hard

The Fiore Family:

Christmas with the Beast * Christmas with the Boss * Christmas
with the Sheriff

Gimme Series:

Sugar * Luck * Rain * Cream * Heat * Love

<u>Holly Hills Christmas:</u>

Holiday's Cookies * Celeste's Secret * Bethany's Crush

<u>The James Family:</u>

No Choice * No Way Out * No More Waiting

<u>Keepsakes:</u>

Keeping Blossom * Keep in Mind

<u>The Lamian Wars:</u>

Bound * Reveal * Release

All Hallows Eve

<u>The Middleton Hotels:</u>

Built for Me * Built to Last * Built Strong

Built Over Time * Built Overnight

<u>Nothing but Trouble Series:</u>

Taking the Bait * Taking the Mafia Princess

<u>The O'Connell Family:</u>

Claiming Red * Burning for Claire

Claiming Abby * Reminding Red

<u>Obsessed Alpha Series:</u>

Stone * Cole * Graham

Theo * Maddox * Alessandro

Tony * Cormack * Cameron

Jake * Sawyer * Liam * Dmitri

<u>Reynolds Ranch Series:</u>

Lara * Tobias

<u>A Rocky Start Series:</u>

Rocky Waters * Her Rock * Rocky Start

<u>A Rough Hands Novella:</u>

My Miracle * Nailing My Wife

Say Something Series:

Say Uncle * Say Please * Say Uncle: Doggy Style

Second Generation:

Say Yes

Seasons of Love:

Wet Summer * Autumn Falls * Winter Frost

Sister Switch:

Testing Her Professor * Assisting Her Boss

A Steele Christmas:

Mason's Winter * Perfectly Wrapped * The Company You Keep

A Steele Fairy Tale:

My Gold * My Forever * My Property * My Prince Charming

A Steele Riders Family Novella Series:

Sammie * Roxie * Mike * Dylan

Steele Riders MC Series:

Boomer * Mick * Jackson * Doc * Beast * Ghost

Wrench * Blade * Boss * Cowboy * Law *Cyber

Steele Riders MC 2nd Generation Series:

Will * Julian* Simon * Miles

Southern Hospitality:

Down South * Gone South

Sweet Temptation Bay:

A Taste Of Honey * The Mayor's Surrender * Trapped with my Stalker

Sweetheart's Treats:

Sweet Surprise * Doctor's Orders, Sweetheart * Sweet Surrender

Twin Sin:

Stalk Me Please * Sinful Intent

White Wolf Ridge Series:

Turner

Wolfe Creek Series:

Wolfe's Den * Beta: Her Alpha

Raging Kane * Written in History

Standalones:

Auctioned to the Kingpin* Buying Love * Christmas Compromise * Conquering Alexandria

Ecstasy Captured * Grant's Deal * Hunted* In Heat * Intense

Killer Abs * Love Discovered * Loving My Neighbor * Lucky Ride

Mrs. Valentine * My Christmas Gift

Rainy Days * Stormy Nights * Red Hot Nights

Room Service * Scarred * Sharp Curves

So Wrong * Standing There

The Mobster's Virgin * The Wedding Guest